I Would Love To End Up With You, But!!!

I WOULD LOVE TO END UP WITH YOU, BUT!!!

ANUP NAIR

PARTRIDGE
A Penguin Company

Partridge books may be ordered through booksellers or by contacting:

Partridge India
Penguin Books India Pvt.Ltd
11, Community Centre, Panchsheel Park, New Delhi 110017
India
www.partridgepublishing.com
Phone: 000.800.10062.62

ACKNOWLEDGEMENT

The scariest part of the whole writing procedure is the section were I thank the people who helped me during the long and struggling journey of writing this book. There were many people who directly and indirectly have been a part of this book. I would want to apologize in advance if I have forgotten to mention any of my dear ones.

The first person who comes to my mind when I think of writing is my beloved grandfather, Mr Gopalan Nair. I am extremely thankful for his exceptional genes which behaved as a catalyst for the growth of the writer within me. I would like to thank my father who showed patience and confidence in the career path that I chose for myself. I would like to thank my best friends Manu & Sheetal for their constant support and encouragement. They were the ones who believed in my journey in the path of writing. Last but not the least; I would like to thank Muralidharan for the fabulous clicks for the cover page.

DAY 1

There were huge cheers when I got on to the stage to deliver my speech. It was not an everyday affair that one passed his graduation with a gold medal. I always had this problem of starting trouble, as I got really anxious on big occasions. The same thing happened, as it was my first speech in front of such a huge gathering. I stood in front of the microphone and was about to give my speech when a loud bell rang. I panicked and was waiting for the noise to subside or else I would forget my speech. I desperately wanted the commotion to stop so that the function could move on. I opened my eyes to find myself staring at a green metal sheet which happened to be the base of the bed above me. It was a double-decker cot. I realized that I had fast forwarded myself four years into the future and added a gold medal to make my dream a bit fancier. My dreams portray my state of mind at that time, urging to get out of that place. A 24*7 counter strike gamer was now in a small town of Tamil Nadu where having water to bathe was a luxury. Anyway, sentiments apart, it was time for college.

As usual, crippled with laziness, I dragged myself out of bed and without caring to switch on the light; I instinctively walked into the bathroom. Here I share my bathroom with five other people, not like the attached bathroom, I had for myself at home. As always I was late for college. One needs some form of encouragement to go to that dump place daily. Encouragement in my case was GIRLS! The life in an engineering college is so boring otherwise, especially when it is a class without girls, like the one I had. There were times when I thought that I would die a virgin in such dump places. I never had a settled life; always travelling like nomads to unknown places, were I hardly could understand the local languages. In order to talk to a girl, one needs to overcome various hurdles. In my case it was my shyness and, to top it all, I could not speak their language well. I would end up being a stand up comedian to them, if I tried talking their language. I desperately wanted to avoid that fate for which I needed to come out of this self created cocoon of mine and start interacting with people. I really wanted to feel how it was to fall in love; the rest was there in my genes.

I used to wake up on hearing the horn of our college bus, waiting outside the hostel gates. Last night I promised to myself not to be late for the first day of college and here I am!! Just ten minutes left for the college bus to leave and I have to choose between bathroom and toilet as I don't have the luxury for both.

I was very good in strategizing stuffs right from the beginning. I chose toilet as it was tough to avail that in our so called college. I somehow dragged myself into the college bus, we (me and my roommates) used to put in our uniform from our hostel rooms and run for the bus with everything from belt to socks in our hands. We never believed in wasting time, so thought we could use the free time in the bus to do the remaining dressing and, somehow, with extreme difficulty we made it to the college. Out of the bus and I saw a construction yard. At first I thought I was at the wrong place but soon I realized that this was the place I was going to spend my next four years. Actually it was a great place for an engineering student; we could see all the live machineries and would get great practical knowledge of a project as we could be part of such a huge project, working on the construction of a college right from scratch. That was the only way I saw of consoling myself. I was not much of an interacting person. The whole idea of coming to south India to study didn't fit in well with me. I had never ever heard of the place called Erode before getting admission in this construction yard (college). I entered my class, along with my roommates and sat somewhere in the middle of the class, as most of the last benches were already occupied. Some of the guys in our class came to me and introduced themselves. They believed I was a crazy alien as they couldn't imagine that some guy would come this far to such a hopeless place to do engineering. But I didn't pay much attention to any of them. The first thing I could make out from the class was that there were no gals in the class. That was the second shocking news I got after stepping down from the bus, the first being my fate to study in this construction yard. There were only two possible guesses: Either I was mad or I was really mad!

The first day went by with this utter shock and meeting some of my classmates and teachers, who were making a great effort as if to learn how to teach. We were like Guiney pigs for them, to have a trial and error session to correct and perfect themselves for future endeavours. The second day, as I reached the corridor, I saw a gal in white, she was hot!!! She was an angel from above, as if god heard my prayers and sent a girl to sooth my eyes. I still don't remember the last time I went to a temple. As every learned man says, you don't have to go to a temple to get blessings like this. It's *karma* and this shows that my ancestors have done something crazy for me to be worth this delight. I examined her for quite a while. She was making her way to the college from the gals' hostel which was next to our college building and this was what my analysis resulted in: She had a spotless brown skin. It was smooth, shiny and SEXY. The nose, though a little blunt, was cute. Her lips, without any lip gloss, glistened with lust. Her sharp curves, together with young unconquered assets, could easily compete with a temptress of a chick flick or an erotic female of Ellora caves. On the outside, she wore a salwar. I was blessed as I could guess her outlines better. In doing so, I felt the torch of civilization revolt between my legs and I would bet that the same would have happened to anyone who could imagine her from the description that I have given. She was much more than one could describe using a pen and paper. I made my way out of the class, to have a peek at what was going on in the other class were she was seated. There was a huge crowd already to have a glimpse of her. All the guys in the class were shocked to find me at the corridor as they usually didn't find me hangout like that.

DAY 7

It had been almost a week since I saw her last, but I had not done anything other than staring at her from different angles. I was like the spy in a James bond movie, sneaking from behind, between the gaps of the classroom doors, behind the canteen doors and what not! I used to take great risks just to have a glimpse of her. In my case I was risking my image and the so called cold attitude. If someone asks me to write a book on her, I might still be able to do so, but just saying a word to her or greet her was turning out to be a mountainous task for me. But I had to act fast, the rules of the jungle also applied in these cases, it was always survival of the fittest and this competition would turn bloody as there were quite a few contenders. I just had two choices—to have a girlfriend in the first year or to celibate for the next four years, which is a pretty long time. I didn't want to end up a despo!!!

Today I saw her passing by the hostel road with her friends, seemed like newbies were getting acquainted to the campus. A friend of mine was walking towards them to have a chat with them. He is always good at these matters so I thought of accompanying him. Staying with him would give me a good chance of getting into their good books. This was a good opportunity to talk to her. There were five of them. They were all talking to him as if they knew each other for centuries, whereas I was standing in the background playing the role of a shrub and discerning whether god had gifted me with a tongue or not. I was virtually invisible to their eyes. I could not muster the courage to speak to them. I was staring at them with infinite blankness or, should I say, I was staring at her!

I was busy admiring her when suddenly she looked at me and told that even I could join there talk. All of a sudden I became the centre of attention and all started laughing. Whatever she said, it wasn't a joke and there was no reason for them to laugh. I just wished I could have some super power through which I could make the others vanish from that place, so that I would have her all to myself. She was not being funny when she said this, but still I was embarrassed. That was really a good start. Just what I didn't want!

The first week of college passed quite fast. It was a Sunday. It was a good respite from the academic stress that I was facing. Our semester started with a bang, our seniors had told that maths this year was tough. On top of that, our professor was of no good either. Those who go to college and never come out are called professors. They spend their first four years getting tortured and the rest of their lives torturing the lives of others.

I was finally back in my room; all my roommates had already arrived. I took time as I was spying around Neha. All had a good time chatting about our day in college and some about their girlfriends. I was so involved in my love fiasco last few days that I never talked much about my friends.

Let me start with Gaurav, in one word he is a psycho!! His problem is that he never listens and is eccentric about sex. Fantasizing about sex is his moral obligation. He relates sex to the most emotional scenes of a movie. In my opinion, he would have been a better sexologist than an engineer. He has the greatest collection of Maxims and debonair. Can say that he was the most popular among guys because of the rare collections he had. Pre orders were taken for his collections and his collections were always on waiting list.

The next is Aakash, he is an emotional *attyachar*. He emotionally blackmails all of us. He always wins an argument or convinces us through his emotional stories, but he is good at heart. He loves his family a lot. That does not mean others don't!! But he is very closely attached to his mother. The third in the list is Aditya. He is a replica of Harish Chandra or his rebirth, to be more specific. Even if the teacher allows us to cheat in the exams he won't do it. In order to succeed in life, either you work hard or you cheat hard. It is hard for the people, stuck in between the two, to succeed. Can you believe that he cannot copy even when asked to? He has never heard of the saying, "Rules are meant to be broken." Then comes the most interesting guy in the lot, Nikhil. He is a real Adonis, he has a persona which consumes anyone approaching him. He is good in studies, sports and famous among gals. He is not that good looking, but manages quite well. Last but not the least was Karthik. There is not much I know about him, but he always has a mobile attached to his ear lobes. He walks with it, he sleeps with it and he even SHITS with it. He does not interact much with any of us, he prefers talking to gals. So we give him his space. He is bit weird to be specific. For the first one year, no one in the room saw him use the toilet or go to the bathroom. He surely respects water a lot. He was a perfect product for the gulf, where water is expensive than oil. But then after a year he changed radically, talking to girls and using the wash room more than once a day. I believe he is making up for the losses of the previous years.

DAY 15

Wanted to leave that day's disaster behind and start afresh and today is the best time to do so. My friend Aditya has invited Neha and her friends out for lunch and I am lucky enough to accompany him. I was madly in love with her or to say crazy about her. I was not sure about love because I never knew what love was. It was not lust. That's because I have never fantasized her. I had planned something for today. I underwent counselling from Aditya. Just accompanying them for lunch won't do the trick; I had to start a conversation. I had to be brave and talk to her. But the very thought of her turns me red. Words just won't come out of my mouth. Thought of starting with friendship but feared that it would end up just in friendship. Anyway, I kept all that aside and took off to the restaurant with my friend Adi. The trip till the restaurant was heroic. We had to travel by the line buses. I had never been in one of them. These things are overflowing with people and almost bent towards one side. By the time I reached the restaurant, I was all drowned in sweat, not just mine but all the people around me in the bus. The combination of sweat with my deodorant gave a new fragrance in the air. The girls were to join us from the restaurant. I was dressed in my favourite black shirt and blue jeans and I must confess the fact that I was looking good till I got into the bus. We all reached the restaurant, it was a good place. Was thinking of bringing her next time around, but just me and her alone. Can say a date! The problem with me is that I imagine too much and create an imaginary world before even keeping the first step. Here I had not even talked to her yet and I was already planning the time and place for a date. I said "hai" to her. My heart was beating at triple its normal rate. It was the first time I had spoken to her. The blood flow in my head had gone up and my ears turned red. She was wearing a black skirt, which was of knee length. She had a cream coloured top with good craft work on it. She really had good dress sense. Her innocent face was glowing with confidence. She looked like an angel that day, which she does look everyday. Her smile was enough to transport me to a dream world. I could not even look at her. I was staring at the wall when I was talking to her. She might have presumed that I had a squint. We were having our food but I was admiring her in between each bite. She wore no make up but still her beauty touched the pinnacle of charm. Long silky lustrous hair, glistering teeth fabricating an impeccable laughter and radiant glow on her face that left me spellbound. My eyes were wide open learning every aspect of her, when suddenly she looked at me. I was frozen as if someone made a statue out of me. My panoptic eyes were glued to her for quite a while. We did not have much of a conversation but I still enjoyed the day. There was not much to talk about, but I loved each and every moment I spent with her.

DAY 21

Back in the hostel, everyday was like a new mission. We used to end up in trouble everyday. We did play many pranks in the hostel. The best one was adding surf in the tetra pack of mango juice and giving it to friends. For the next few hours there was a huge crowd in front of the toilet. Once they were empty, they all formed a crowd in front of our room with glass full of detergent. But like always, we made a great escape. There were many instances when we had to spend our nights under the open sky in front of some restaurants or shops. We made a good bonding with the street dogs of that area, because of our forced outdoor camping at night. In the college the past few days have been pretty boring, nothing special!

I have described everything about her, everything that I knew!! I have been avoiding her for the past few days, not because there was any change in my feeling

towards her. I didn't want myself to be portrayed as
a despo_that obviously I am! People call it attitude,
but I needed time to overcome my fear. I was getting
mentally prepared for the meeting.

But what I heard today was heart breaking. Adi told
me that she was dating some other guy in her home
town, some crush from her school days. All the words,
uttered by Adi, were arrows poisoned at the tip with
envy. I had to accept it as I knew Adi would not joke
about this matter. They just hit me hard and deep. I
stood still hearing this, but I felt as if an earth quake
just hit and world around me was shaking. I didn't
go for dinner that night; I excused myself by faking a
headache. I thought of it all the night and that brought
a whirlwind in my mind and that made me sick. Sitting
on my bed, with the room absorbed in stark darkness,
I was staring at the ceiling fan. I think I cried, or can
say a few droplets came from my tear glands. I hate to
accept that I cried. But I did!!!!!! I had never felt this sad.
I was crying as if I had a breakup. It had been fifteen
days since I met her for the first and all I had managed
to say was a hai! Great going buddy!! What else could I
have expected then, she might not even know my name.
All I knew was that I loved her and had already started
seeing dreams of me and her together. These school days
really suck, mine actually did suck but girls shouldn't be
allowed to love or like a guy at that tender age. Guys
from outside should be given a fair chance to try out
their luck, which I was deprived of. I was really losing
my mind and started creating a rule book for love.

DAYS TO COME . . . .

I lost track of days after that day's incident or news, to be more specific. I lost track of almost everything. Exams were approaching. I tried my best to concentrate and managed to pass in a few of them. Everyone, in our class, took it as an achievement to brag about the number of subjects they failed in their first year. I couldn't even top those rankings as I turned out to be an average, who passed half of his subjects, neither a stud nor a book worm. The first year of college was over. Apart from the Neha fiasco, rest of the year was good, had some crazy time with friends, had a great interaction with seniors in the form of ragging, fought with students from other departments and enjoyed some gang fights in the campus, all the usuals for a classic college life. I also managed to get a suspension for fighting, which I could brag about among friends, but kept it a secret from my family. I didn't feel that my result along with the suspension would be entertained by them by any means. I didn't want to spoil my vacation either. But thoughts of her tormented me always. I was sick and tired of myself. I didn't know what it would take me to forget her. Everyone doesn't get what they desire. But who decides all these things? I eagerly wanted someone to tell me what was so special in that boy which made her fall for him. It was just the advantage he had of meeting her first. I really shouldn't complain as I never gave it a try. I just believed the words of a third person and lost all hopes and moved on. I should have at least expressed myself in front of her, which I didn't do and now I feel it's too late. If its destiny then it's fucking playing with me, it's all a game for him and his sadistic sense of humour. I really want to forget her and move ahead but all my confidence gets punctured when I see her. And I would be seeing her for the next three years. I need to move on. I should see it as a boxing bout with a round of four and I have lost the first round, but I still have three more to go. All is not over till it is over.

I left for home the next day after college. We had two long months of leave. After that we would come back as seniors. By the time I hope to overcome all my traumas!

ANJANA

In one word, if I had to explain Anurag, then the first thing that would come to my mind would be "KID." I still don't remember why I used to and still call him kid. But that's how it's stored in my phone too. He is my best friend from the college. When I say best friend, people would imagine something like the bollywood movie types in which you hang out with one other the whole time and always seen in each others company. But things were different between me and Anurag. We were best friends who rarely talked to each other, we only communicated with each other through messages. Thanks to all crazy packages given by certain mobile service providers in the state, we had the liberty to send one hundred free messages through our phone daily. But it was not something like an instantaneous click and best friends forever type of a start. We didn't talk to each other during most of

our first year. We started talking to each other during
the end of the first year. We always knew each other
through Aditya. Aditya belonged to my hometown and
we both knew each other well and I knew Anurag as
Aditya's full of attitude room mate and a cold hearted
friend. I always thought of the reason why Anurag never
used to talk to me while in the college. He made sure
that he didn't even give a smile. Smile was a difficult
expression in Anurag's dictionary and it was a rare sight
and so I couldn't complain regarding that. In the end,
I zeroed down to two possibilities for his behaviour. It
was either because he was very shy or his attitude never
allowed him to go to someone and talk. He had a very
bad image in the college. People used to complain of his
lack of interaction and coldness towards people around
him. But those talks or rumours about him didn't
affect our friendship. It grew to a very strong bond.
We created a new record in messaging; it was evident
from my phone keypad as none of the keys were visible
because of the constant messaging. The only time we
didn't message was when we were sleeping; we even
started using the phone during class hours. It made up
for the cold shoulders he used to show in the college.
I was very much aware of his behaviour and attitude
towards people. People often used to wonder as to why
I was hanging out with him or even staying in contact
with him. But I felt good in his company and I felt he
was the best round there for me. He was stubborn and
egoistic to the core, he always made sure that he got
what he wanted and he would thrive till he got that. I
used to be part of the crime even though I knew it very
well that whatever he was asking for was unreasonable.
I never said no to any of the requests or demands that

he put forward. I could never justify my stand to him but then, that was the beauty of our friendship. The description I have about him doesn't sound like that of a best friend material but he was actually nice at heart. But with time, I felt that during some instances, things were getting out of hand and at some point I did draw a line because I could not keep supporting him at the cost of getting myself hurt.

Anurag did prove everyone wrong and answered to all the critics when I was hospitalized. He made sure that he was present beside me all the time. When the time came, he didn't shy away or show his regular attitude. Anurag was not an emotional kind of a guy, he was as everyone describes, cold and blunt. He always made decisions which were practical and always had reasoning to all the decisions that he took. He always had a clear idea as to what to do in life and career. His life was a time table which had no flexibility or consideration for anyone. He was never comfortable with the people around him, even his so called friends or roommates, probably because he was from another part of the world. People in north India have their own definition of fun and socializing. It takes time for a person to cope up with a new surrounding after he has spent major part of his life elsewhere. But I feel he started making exceptions later on in life and I was one of them. It was as if he tested the people around him and only the proven were allowed to cross the invisible wall he had created around him. Most of the people around him thought the wall to be part of his attitude and distanced themselves from him. He was very much dependent on me during this self isolation phase of his life. He used to curse every day his so called wrecked life in south. But I tried my maximum to console him and make him feel at home and I loved this responsibility of mine. The feeling that he considered me this close was touching all together.

LOVE AGAIN OR
IS IT . . . . ?????

Time has finally come for our juniors to arrive. We all stood at the passage blocking there way. All had there style of impressing the freshers. I just accompanied my friends, wasn't much interested in knowing any of them. I was more interested in handing my assignments to any of the gals with good hand writing. All gals do have good hand writing. It was my chance of submitting assignments on time. Our staffs had a good strategy of teaching all the easy portions and the one's which they didn't understand were usually given as assignment. I selected a gal from the group, which was making its way from the college hostel, dressed in red. She looked good, so I assumed that she might even write well. She was a little dark, soft curly hair, which hung around her face. She had round buttocks and generous love handles. She had nice firm assets. She was cute which suited her looks. My ability to scan and examine is good as ever. She was very soft spoken; it might be just because I was her senior, a token of respect from her side. I handed my assignment sheets and she took it without any complaints. She completed everything by evening and returned the papers. I started liking this way of ragging. For the first time in my college life, I got my assignments completed on time and with excellent presentation. She actually had great hand writing. I did the same next day, gave all my pending assignments to the same gal, even the day after. But today I saw tears in her eyes and when asked the reason, she cried and left with my book. Later I came to know that there were other seniors who made her do the same work. She was overloaded with others' work. I did pity her. I did have a soft corner for her as she looked innocent and she was doing all my work with at most sincerity. The next day, I met her alone; she completed my assignments as always. I helped her tackle the other guys who used to make her do their work, but still she was doing mine. I started seeing her on a regular basis. Sometimes just to chat, soon we became good friends, all the other seniors knew that I had a soft corner for her, so they all abided by the bro code and left her alone. It was like a mutual respect the seniors had for each other when it comes to ragging. We never used to fight over a girl and try to embarrass ourselves in front of them.

Lying on my bed on the same day, I thought about this new gal in my life or, to be specific, in the college, the assignment gal or better known as 'Shreya'. I tried to distance myself from her but I ended up appreciating and liking her appearance, her artistic eyes, soft ears and slender neck. Oh God!! What the hell am I telling!!!

I just could not control myself from telling so. I didn't jerk off thinking about her. I had high respect for her; just one question rang my head "can I fall in love all over again??" I really don't know why I define my infatuation to Neha as love, moving that out of the equation, I can very well say that Shreya can be my first love, but like every other time, I am just coming to conclusions too soon. If all planets were fit for living, then earth would have lost its unique identity. Likewise, if I fall in love with every other gal I meet, then love would loose its meaning or in easier terms, people would loose faith in my definition of love. It would be same as lust and greed. The question which haunts my mind is whether I deserve her. If yes then what about my love for Neha?? Was it true?? I still can't get her out of my mind, then how could I even think of any other gal!!! I wasn't really in love. I was really desperate to be in a relationship. I was not even trying to know her well. I just wanted to forget Neha and I chose the wrong way to do it. I should have at least let Neha know about what was there in my heart. It would have made me feel better; it would have helped me on with my life.

GOING BY MY INSTINCT!

A few days later, I told Shreya about my feelings for her or I can say, I was forced to say because of the circumstances created by my friends. They did spread rumours in the college that I liked Shreya, which was true. Finally, these rumours reached Shreya and I had to confront her on the topic. No one forced me to, but I did, I should have given one more thought before doing so. During the next few days we used to come early to college and traipsed the entire college campus. I told her about my past (but not about my feelings for Neha) and she told me about hers. One thing I noticed about Shreya_was that she talked a lot and I was just looking at her eyes and listening to all that she said. She was a determined gal, making a life in the world where the rules have been written by men who keep changing the rules of the game as per their convenience and which favour them. We used to talk in the college all day and even on phone after reaching back. She had so much to say, that too with avid excitement. I thought, she was forced to suppress her feelings till then and she was finally liberated. I was very open with her, I felt as if whatever I did or told in front of her didn't matter as she would never misunderstand me. God!! Am I so lucky? It happens in an instant that one falls in love. This just wakes up the philosopher in me, though life fucks everyone for sure but not in every hole! This might not be the kind of philosophy one would expect but I believe in conveying the message and if in this modern era, Bull crap philosophy is what it takes to convey the message to today's generation then so be it.

I just closed my eyes and was thinking of the incidents of the past few weeks and suddenly a face came to my mind, it was Neha's!!! I was really sick and tired of myself. I really wanted to know as to what it would take for me to forget her. Deep in my heart, I was feeling like a cheat. What ever be the reason, I won't be able to tell these things to Shreya. It would surely hurt her and I was not willing to do that. What the hell is wrong with my character?? I had dragged a girl into this relationship; she never forced anything on me. It was my responsibility to stand up to my commitment.

A few months back, I was in love with Neha and now I claim to be in love with Shreya. What is the guarantee that I won't fall for any third gal?? The way things are going for me, I can't even guarantee that. I have really screwed myself up. I think I was not ready for this relationship. But this is not the time to think of all this. It's too late, I should have thought of this earlier. Now I won't hurt her, I hope so . . . .

MY FIRST DATE

I thought of meeting her after our first internal exams, I meant a date. Talking about dates, never before in my academic history had I performed so badly. I was very much confident of flunking in mathematics this year. Even the professor had the same confidence in me. It was for the first time that both of us came to a mutual agreement on an issue. I bet even he would have flunked the exam if he was made to write the same, so we can't be blamed for this. But this won't stop me from meeting Shreya this Sunday if she agrees. I called her and asked her out for lunch. She thought for some time and said yes. It's a typical gal thing. They would be waiting for the guy to ask them out. But when we do so, they would show the reluctance and expect us to ask again and again, which we do. It was not just a meet; it was an official date after we started seeing each other.

I reached the restaurant well before time; I am very particular and cautious when it comes to these things. It's not that I have done this before. She finally arrived. I had asked her to wear her red dress. I really love her in it. She looks good in all the dresses, but red is special for me, that's the dress in which I saw her for the first time. We did share a hidden chemistry—hidden for both of us. I was about to take her to the restaurant when she asked weather we could go for a walk. I felt it to be a better idea to share my feelings with her. It would be a bit romantic. After an exhaustive walk we decided to sit at some place. So we thought of returning to the restaurant. We took a corner seat, she was sitting beside me. I was all smiles. We sat there and talked quite a lot. To be more specific, she talked a lot and I was listening. All her friends complain that she does not talk much but I felt the opposite, she talks too much which I liked very much. It compensated for my not so talkative nature. I could sit there and listen to her all day. I can't keep my eyes open for an hour when the professors teach. But this was altogether a different experience. Somewhere in between, she would stop talking and wave her hand, so as to check whether I was sleeping with my eyes open. That's when I would realize that I had been staring at her for quite a long time. After having lunch we took off from the restaurant and started walking towards the street. That was when the unimaginable happened. She just held my hand while walking. WOW!!!!!!! That was one hell of a feeling. No words to express it. Totally speechless!!! From there we walked till my bike, hand in hand. There were people staring at us but we weren't bothered. I hoped to drop her in her hostel but her friends were waiting for her somewhere nearby. This wish of mine remained unfulfilled. Anyway, I had a great time, one of the best in my life till date.

WITH FRIENDS

Exams started. The chilling climate at this time hardened our asses and made it difficult for us to sit and study. As usual we all were up to the last day study and there was hell lot to study. I started studying energetically, but later drowsiness took charge of my body, and eyes automatically got shut down. I had a very good nap and I woke up around twelve at night. I was very much freaked out. There was very less time and so much to study. I spent most of the time this semester talking to Shreya on phone till midnight and chatting with friends. I had no other option than going for Plan B. Stop this hard work and go for smart work. In other words "Bit". Nikhil was the best person to consult in this matter. I spent the whole night preparing bits along with him. We were partners in crime when it came to our so called smart work.

Finally the day of exam arrived, undoubtedly the most atrocious day in anybody's college life. It was a complete havoc in the room. Gaurav was shouting with tooth paste in his mouth. Even Nikhil was shouting from outside the bathroom door. Aakash had entered the bathroom with the text book an hour back. I knew very well that he wouldn't come out until he was done with his revision. On one side, there were us who couldn't even complete the portions once, and were having a life support in the form of tiny bits of paper stuffed inside our pants, shirts and god knows were all, and on the other side we had Aakash with his third or fourth turn of revision. So it was best for me to skip the morning routine. I hope this sacrifice would show up in my exam results. The exams were ok, I applied all the risk taking manoeuvres and used up all the resources I had. Nikhil was very good in this. He knew very well which questions would come and which would not. We saw Aakash after the exam; his face was swollen as if bit by a honeybee. That's when we came to know about his morning fiasco. He slept for almost an hour in the loo and the mosquitoes ate up his face and butt. We laughed a lot on this. People around us thought we were laughing at them. So we turned silent and moved out before they turned our faces swollen. The exams went on one by one. None of them was great, courtesy to the late night phone calls and sleep attack during the morning. Aakash was given special attention when he was in loo. The whole examination was like a roller coaster ride for us, providing bumps and jerks all through the way and finally into the water. That's when the marks are announced. But I do like this time of the year when we have exams. That's the time we spend the maximum time with our friends. Examination hall is the place where you see the perfect unity, passing of bits, showing answer sheets and what not. We try our maximum to get through the papers and we also make sure that the one sitting next to us also does the same. That's one thing you would never see anywhere else . . . .

A TASTE OF INTIMACY

Exams over and it was time to go home and guess what? I wasn't alone this time. Shreya was coming with me. We both happen to be from the same place. We thought of going by the train at night. Both of us reached separately and met at the station. We reached a few hours early as our train was at night. Both of us entered the station and wandered here and there, until we found a place to sit alone. It's difficult to find such a place in the railway station. We sat there hand in hand and talked for a while. Then we thought of going to some place else. We kept our luggage in the cloak room and left. We found a good place nearby. It was a garden, other than some old ladies coming for evening walk, there were only a few couples present. The weather had taken a swift turn and was setting the mood of intimacy. We walked through the fragrant muddy tracks, crossing the gardens to the woods. We walked through the woods, talking about what? That I didn't have a clue at the moment as there was a lot that Shreya spoke and it was hard to keep track of all that stuff. We were trying to find a perfect place to sit. Finally we found a small hillock nearby. There were trees all around, so we were virtually invisible to the outside world. The aroma of the surroundings seduced my heart and the sudden advent of clouds in the sky added colour to my emotions. Besides all that, it was Shreya's eyes that were drawing me towards her. Both of us climbed the hillock and sat there. I could feel it was the moment, the first moment of intimacy, might be the moment of my first kiss, it all depends on how Shreya responded, didn't want to hurry as that first kiss could easily turn in to my first slap. I was a bit sweaty and the situation was making it worse. I wanted to use my deo but it was in my bag and a mint to go with that would have been good as I was very much positive about a kiss. But I didn't want her to guess my intentions, so I didn't go for the mint. Hoping the fragrance of the surroundings would dissolve my body odour away, I was preparing myself for what was going to be an intense moment. Excited, nervous and little cautious, I tried to be as gentle as possible. I closed the gap between us and put my arms around her. She was behaving very shyly, her personality saw a radical change all of a sudden. She transformed into a shy traditional young Indian bride waiting for her groom to unravel the scarf on her face. She showed no resistance at all, she was ready for whatever I was to do. As if there was no one else on this planet other than two of us, I approached her and she closed her eyes. I held her palms and pulled her towards me, the rest was history, something which would be really unexplainable for a rookie like me. I might be able to explain it better, once I turned good at it and as for now I was really busy enjoying the moment rather than looking for words to express it.

BETRAYAL

It's been a month since I came home for vacations. The big news for this semester is that I haven't yet called Shreya or picked her call. She has been calling me all day long, but I have been keeping the phone ringing. Don't ask me why, but I wanted to get out of this relationship. It was as if the Gemini in me was speaking. It was the effect of the twin personality of Gemini. Was it only a one night stand for me? Was I using her? By the look of things that have passed, it sure looks that way. All these questions ran through my mind the whole day. I had no right to blame my zodiac sign for the uncanny behaviour I had done. What the hell would she think about me? I was using her for that one night. Am I that kind of a person or is it NEHA? Is she still tormenting my mind? I should have given a fucking thought about it before I made out with Shreya. Right now I am trying to escape and giving stupid

justifications which are hard even for me to believe.
Then how the hell can I expect Shreya to fall for it? To
be frank, I really loved Shreya, but the only problem is
that I was not completely over with my craze for Neha
and this fascination was driving me away from Shreya.
I was comparing her with Neha in each and every
matter. Should I talk to her again or is it too late for
that? By now she might have got a clear picture of me.
If someone asks her to explain about me in a word then
"SCOUNDREL" would be the least she would say. I
sent her a message the next day. I don't want to disclose
the exact content of the message but that was the last
I heard from her. I made sure that I ended it the most
pathetic manner I could. Shreya's chapter was closed.
Easy said and done or is it??? With all those questions
in mind, I returned to college for my next semester. She
was not the only one who had some asking to do. Two
of my closest friends knew about this relationship. One
was Aditya, my roommate, and the other was Anjana,
my best friend. Haven't yet told you people about her.
She is the one with whom I share all the happenings
in my college and home. She is all in one, my friend,
my P. A. and everything. Don't have words to describe
her. Can say, she knows more about me and my family
than I know. Shocking??? Even I was!!! She, along with
Aditya, had an important role to play in my relationship
with Shreya. She was the mediator for me. So, obviously
she had loads of questions to ask and I did owe her
an explanation. More than Anjana, it was Shreya who
deserved respect and proper justification. I did talk to
Anjana about it but it was least satisfactory. I expected
that! But there was nothing she could do to change my
mind; she knew that and so she never tried. Anjana was

blaming herself for what happened because she was equally involved in getting the two of us together. I came to know that Shreya was more upset with Anjana and Aditya but not with me. The particular statement from her was really touching, but I was really holding myself back from approaching her again. Even Aditya was pizzed with my attitude. They came to a conclusion that I didn't value relationship and love. Somewhere in the back of my mind, I knew that I was going to pay for what I did to Shreya. Anjana always called me a KID. I just proved her right with my kiddish attitude. In the times to come, the most difficult part for me in the college would be to come face to face with Shreya. It was so very difficult for me to look into her face. It just made me pathetic. She would boldly look into my face which would make me realize that I was a big time looser. By the time it was a talking point in college that I broke up with Shreya. These people need something to talk over an evening coffee. What better to talk about than their friends' break up. They would make up their own stories as to what would be the reason behind it. One can add yet another chapter to my so called fucked up life. I wasn't upset about what people talked about me, but I was really hurt to hear things that were spoken about Shreya. She had really nothing to do in the matter; I dragged her, left her and now defamed her. Everything was done as per my convenience and my state of mind. I proved the opinion about me in college that I did not care about people's feelings and I was a cold hearted mean person. I was really left speechless at that moment.

MY DARK LIFE

My life turned dull in the absence of Shreya. I used to be on phone the whole night but now I didn't have any use of phone. The only phone call I had was from my mom, who made it a point to call me everyday from the day I left home. This was the time when I learned the importance of friends. They stood by me even though they knew that I was wrong. During these days, they were of great help to me. That is why it's said, "A faithful friend is the medicine for life." My college life had turned boring, had nothing else to do other than spend time in the class and pray that I didn't come across Shreya. It was the time when I turned my concentration back on studies. Had a lot to cover, as I had flunked in almost all the subjects that I wrote. That was because I was too much involved in Shreya and everything around her. It's her absence that made me realize her importance. Love is a temporary madness.

It erupts like a volcano and then subsides. It's when it subsides that you have to make the decision. I can say, that's when I made my decision or can say the blunder that I made. Have you ever thought why people close their eyes when they kiss? Even I did so, but never knew the reason behind it till date. It might be because some of the greater things in life are unseen. That is why we close our eyes when we kiss, cry or dream. All that had happened in the last few months, were like a roller coaster ride. Just as what Socrates said, "Hottest love has the coldest end." I self destructed my love to get hurt in the long run. The hardest thing is to see your love, love someone else. That is what I had to see, Shreya with someone else. In one way it was good as she got some support in those difficult times. Finally the guilt in me of leaving Shreya alone was subsiding. I had done nothing for that, it was the new support she got in life and a good one. He is a good guy as far as I know. This last one year of my college life began with a smile. Grew with a kiss and ended with a tear drop . . . .

ADDICTION

Exam went quite well. Compared to the previous ones this one was great. This time, back home, I had my thinking cap on. Shreya with another guy and Neha still stuck with the same guy. I needed to move on. In the past few weeks I learned new habits. My liking towards alcohol had increased to a new level. I liked the drugged semi conscious effect. I was doing all the possible things which I should not be doing and there was no one to stop me. I started smoking, hadn't quite got hold of it but still managed it ok. I was doing all the cheesy *Devdas* trends which I used to make fun off once. It wasn't that I was in a bad company; no one forced me to do anything. All this was my own wish. The feeling of losing everything was filling my heart and making me realize that I was a loser. Nowadays I even fight with Anjana. All our conversations ended up in a fight. We fought, and I blasted her with all the pathetic words, and she kept listening. Hats off to her, she never took our fights seriously, but she never forgets it either. She brings the topic back at the right time that is one advantage that a girl has in a fight. A girl never forgets the conversation they have during a fight, they use it when they feel that they are losing a fight and the guy would be totally clueless, as he has no idea as to when he spoke those words. A guy expresses himself as a part of that particular moment, whether it is expressing his love or an argument. He tells stuffs and forgets it. But girls have it all stored in their hard disk, that is why god gave them more of grey matter in their brains. They have so much of useless stuffs to store in there. I even formed distance with Adi. I used to tell him everything and get suggestions from him, but now I feel that I even cheated him and so thought of keeping distance from him. I had gone silent and away from the group. We talked less. Everything was coming down right in front of me, and no one to blame other than me. I was screwing myself up. In the midst of all this, our industrial visit was announced. It was a trip to Kodaikanal and Pondicherry. The name given to the trip "Industrial Visit" is to cover up the actual intention of the students which is booze and fun. We usually choose some of the fancy tourist place as industrial visit and select some small scale industry where we spend an hour or two, and then spend the rest of the day in a semi conscious hallucinated phase. Majority of the class was there this time around. First I declined the offer but later agreed as my roommates forced me to do so. Even I felt that it would be a good change and refreshment from my *Devdas* behaviour. If I can't do away with my *Devdas* behaviour then I could always turn to the cheaper alcohol for my so called rescue, as we were going to Pondicherry. This would help me mourn in an economical manner and yet continue my hallucinated state. Whatever reason I tried to give, in order to convince myself, the bottom line was that I was going.

FUN

Our industrial visit was great. I drank and slept, then again woke up and drank till I slept. Things went on like that. It was more of a bar visit than an industrial visit. This might lead me to the rehab or to a medic but you need to learn to live life on the edge or else you are taking too much of space. This way of life gave me an awesome feeling, drugged like hell. We did visit some beautiful places during the course of the trip, but don't remember any of them. We took a week long leave before attending college again. This was the time I got introduced to a gal named Radhika through net. Here we go again; I know what you people would be thinking. Yes, you are right! It's not my fault that I fell for her, she trapped me. I saw her picture, and the first thing my heart said, 'enough of the mourning, lets get back to business.' I was a regular guy on social networking sites; it was the only means by which I used to keep in touch with my friends back home. One day I saw a friends request from this gal called Radhika. I went through her profile details and it suggested that she hailed from my home town and she was a year younger to me. I was sure that I didn't know her. But still I accepted her request as she was good looking. It's not everyday that a guy like me gets a friends request from a gal like her. She might have got the wrong guy, anyway well for me. I accepted the request and went on with my work hoping that I would get her online some day. I wanted to polish my art of flirtation. It is the art of keeping intimacy at a safe distance. It's the art of giving attention without intention, as far as I know all women love flirts, but some are restrained by shyness and some by senses. The next day I went online every one hour as to make sure that I didn't miss her. I didn't know her timings. It was around four in the evening that I got it right. She was online. It excited me!

ANJANA

I saw a different Anurag during our second year in college, a new and more socializing Anurag, but this Anurag was meant for someone else. It was meant to grab attention of someone else and that someone else was Shreya. Shreya was our junior who belonged to the same hometown as Anurag. His fondness for her grew and this particular fondness slowly evolved to love. It was Anurag's first college love. Being Anurag's best friend, I tried a lot for their relationship. I used to be Anurag's communication medium in the hostel as we both were in the same hostel. I used to make sure that Shreya didn't get ragged in the hostel. In the college, she was left out from the ragging as many knew about her and Anurag. I was really happy for him and their relationship. It really went well for sometime but things fell apart all on a sudden. A trip back home during semester break and what I heard is that Anurag broke up. I never really understood the reason and logic behind his decision, but I was really pizd with his decision as even I was involved in this matter. I had the right to know the complete matter but as it's Anurag, one can expect anything. The situation became a mess and all his friends were made to do the rectifying duty. This led all of us into the bad books of Shreya. I realized one thing after that, Anurag could not take stress in a relationship. He gets exited and goof up things pretty bad. The biggest of his negatives is his anger and it always messes up the situation. He better do something about his anger before it ruins his life and make him do something, which he would repent for life and wouldn't be able to take back. He had to put in a lot of effort, but we managed to handle Shreya.

The good thing about the breakup was that it brought out the lighter side of Anurag. It showed the emotional side of him. He realized his mistake and apologized to Shreya for that. Shreya also felt better seeing the apologetic side of Anurag. Shreya still loved Anurag and she always will. It was Shreya's first true love; no one can blame her for that. Everyone in the friends circle was amazed by the change in Anurag and the gesture that he showed towards her. Anurag made sure to keep in touch with her, and they are good friends now. It was anyway too late for a patch up, as there was that special guy around Shreya who took care of her during the entire trauma she was going through, and supported her through all the hardships. Even Anurag believed that it was he who deserved her more than anyone else.

The best part of our relationship was that we respected each other. We both had our own misunderstandings, fights and arguments, but it only strengthened our relationship. Only his close ones know how caring he is, Anurag finds it very difficult to express his care or love but he shows it when required. He always reaches out to the people close to him and helps them out whole heartedly. He has only very few friends, but he keeps them in his heart. He takes time to know and trust people around him. I was a clear example for that, it took almost a year for Anurag to trust me and open up to me.

The thing that upset me the most was his habit of forgetting things. He never payed much importance to small matters like calling up someone to wish him or her during the birthdays. He used to do it through messaging, which did upset me a lot. To some point, I even got happy with his messages as he even forgot that. The reason to be upset is simple, I considered him to be my best friend and, as a friend, I expected at least a call from him on my birthday. But for Anurag, it was just like another day. Even his birthday's were being celebrated once he joined our company and that's what made him celebrate others birthday too. He made up for all his lame behaviours during the last birthday of my college life. It was totally unexpected as Anurag lied to me that he was going home, that too a day before my birthday. But he surprised me by organising a birthday party in a coffee shop in the city, and also became the first person to have ever gifted me with a bouquet. It is something I would always cherish and remember. This was a clear sign of a new Anurag, an evolved one. It was something our friendship made possible and I am proud of that. I kept the bouquet near me the whole day. It's not an everyday thing that people gift you flowers.

Anurag taught me a new way of being friends. Our friendship started in the most unusual way and goes on like that till date. He liked Neha from day one, but never accepted it. I knew it right from the beginning. But I didn't want to question him on that, as he would tell you something only when he feels comfortable, and as he didn't tell me anything, it was evident that he didn't want to. He was always fascinated towards beautiful girls. It is never a surprise among guys. For Anurag, looks always mattered, it was among his list of priorities. And Neha fulfilled his list pretty well, as she was the college beauty. But he always made sure that he portrayed himself as a Neha hater in front of others. He used abusive words against her when her name came in between our discussions. I always used to imagine the reason why, but things were evident once I came to know about his feelings for her. He never dared to tell her that, mostly because of the fear of a rejection which he was confident about. I believe that is love, which he believed was an infatuation as he found it hard to believe that he loved someone who hated her that time. I used to discuss with Anurag the things that people in her friends circle felt about her, but he was never much bothered about what people felt about him. He was a bit of self centric person at that time. The same has happened with me, when I had issues with people in the college, which I usually had, he used to always shout at me and blame me for the happening. I never used to understand this behaviour of his. It's always my guess that he would have been showing the anger he had on them to me because he never wanted to get into an open fight for me, because most of the fights that I had was with his classmates. As in the college we never used to talk, it was obvious that he would not stand for me there. I always asked him not to judge me from what others say about me. Anurag used to get influenced by people around him, mostly by friends as he trusted them so dearly. Such influences sometimes reflected on his actions and some of the decisions he took over time.

Our fights sometimes turned so ugly that there were times when we didn't talk to each other for even a month. A month doesn't seem huge for many, but one has to consider that we are talking about two people who talked almost twenty four hours a day. I still don't have a clue for his weird behaviour, might be some family problem. He usually tells me about them, but this might be an exception from his side or it is something else which I still don't know. Somehow I never liked his feelings for Neha. I was a bit possessive and jealous regarding him, but now when I think about it, it was something to laugh about. It is funny considering that I and Neha are best friends. We did have our differences during the college days but it's something to laugh about now.

A NEW BEGINNING

As days passed by, our talks increased. It progressed from social networking chats to phone calls and then visits during holidays. Even Radhika managed time for this self obsessed jerk a.k.a Anurag. Yah!! That's me. I knew her very well now and felt that she had special feelings for me. But on the other hand, I never thought of her anything other than a friend. She has been a person to whom I could share my feelings and joy, a person who helped me out of my trauma. She is very much charming and has everything in the right proportion, but she is just not the one. She is just not like Neha. I don't want to bluff anymore. I just don't need a time pass. I had already broken a heart, punished myself to the limit, and here I am again thinking of a similar relationship. Radhika was nice and I couldn't hurt her and so had to be cautious this time. We both had formed a good bond as friends, and I wanted to be a good friend. But that doesn't sound that good. Girlfriend is cool but girl ju1st friend is weird. Slowly I changed my approach towards her, even she sensed that. I purposely decreased our frequency of chats and slowly ended it. To be frank, the only reason I did that was because I was scared of relationship. More than relationships, I was scared about my unpredictable behaviour. My mood swings are unpredictable and it hurts a chain of people related to me at that moment. I had no intention of adding her to the already lengthy chain. I am not the kind of stud who does all these bitchy things and then moves on. I start regretting things and this regret eats me up. So I was no way ready for a regret ride as of now. This over cautious attitude of mine might have driven me away from a genuine affair or a person who was actually meant for me, but I was not in a state to experiment and so thought of concentrating on some more important matters such as studying. My semester exams were coming near, so I thought of keeping these daily sop events out of my mind and concentrate on a bigger trauma, my engineering books. The only time of the day when I touch those books are at night. It helps you get a good night sleep. They are of good help during the hot summer nights, as our city had almost six hours of power cuts. Power cuts were something new for me as I was not faced by something like that in my home town, but two years in this junkyard has made me adapt to this prehistoric lifestyle. I had my own air conditioning for these circumstances, two lines from my engineering books and that's it!!! You are in the dream world. But this time around, I have taken up the book for a different reason, the actual purpose of studying. I had done fairly well in my last semester exams; I cleared most of my lagging papers. I wanted to clear them all this semester. I had bigger goals in life. Flirting with gals is not my only aim in life. But that doesn't mean that I am going to work hard. I work smart. This is one great thing that I have learned from this college and my classmates. It does really work. The other important lesson that I have learned is to care about others. I really never bothered what my actions and speech would do to others. What and how they would feel. I was a selfish jerk. I am not telling that I have improved a lot but things are changing. Anjana has some role to play in that, even Adi has. But most important are my experiences in the past two years. Mainly with Shreya, A spoiled brat wanting to improve, trying to be a good friend, a person whom others can trust. It's not at all easy for a guy like me, but two more years in the company of these great friends would do the trick. There are important things in life other than love and lust.

THE SECOND HALF

The beginning of the next semester promised better things for me. I stopped thinking about Neha and Shreya for the time being. Neha would always have a special place in my heart. It would be an untold love story. A one sided affair. I have never been able to express my love for her, nor will I do it in the future. This is my way of loving her. Call it madness as most of them would think so. But most importantly, I am happy with this madness. I started interacting more with friends and classmates. I try my max not to hurt them with my sharp words but not with Anjana. I always hurt her with my action and words. I don't mean to, but I end up doing so. College days were turning out to be boring with all the assignments which now I had to do by myself, too much of stress with the semester exams and the loads of papers I was lagging. But these things never came in between our enjoyment. Bunking classes was on full flow, even got suspended for ragging, which I am proud of. One day, all of a sudden, I got a forward message from an unknown number. Whenever I get such unknown messages I send the number to Anjana for cross checking. What she told me shocked me completely. It was Shreya!!! I was very much happy getting her message. I had been very rude to her and even the breakup went all wrong. I always wanted to call her and apologize, but never had the strength to do that. But now I got a good opportunity to repent. I called her back to the same number and asked, "Who is this?? I got a message from this number!!!" There was no reply from the other side; I could listen to the heavy breathing. "You don't even remember me" was the reply from the other side. I asked the question again and that was the end of the conversation. She cut the call. I thought for quite a while, asked Anjana for her opinion and finally thought of calling her again. The phone rang for quite a while, as soon as she took the call, I started speaking, "I do know who this is, I was just confirming." "I can't forget you this fast Shreya." I continued. There was a long pause and then I asked "how you doing? It's been quite a long time!" "It's been a long hard time for me, I am not as easy going as you are and I still don't understand this time pass relationship. I am not as intelligent as you are!!" Shreya said. I knew very well that she needed answers and I felt that she deserved to know the truth. But what do I tell her?? Why did I dump her?? Even I don't have the answer for that. But she won't leave me without an explanation. "I needed time before going into a serious relationship, I made a mistake proposing you without thinking of all this. I was not ready for a relationship. I know I cheated on you. But it wasn't a time pass for me. I did love you but I needed time and some space. I hope you understand." I said. "I was the one who always had to understand and suffer; you were always true in your own terms. Where did I go wrong??" Shreya asked. I didn't know what to say. The only thing she had done wrong was trusting me. I was ready to do anything to apologize. "You have done nothing wrong; I am ready to anything so that you can forgive me." I said. There was a long pause again, heavy breathing again. Then I heard something which shocked me further. "Can you be like what you were to me a year back? Can you come back?" she asked. I very well knew that she was happy with her new partner, and, as far as I heard, he was very caring. I had to be very careful this time. The situation involved more than life. I was a little tempted to go back to her. But I can't and I shouldn't. I lost my chances and I shouldn't be interfering in their happy life. I just took hold of the situation and made her understand. I wanted her to be my friend, but I knew the fact that "a friend can become a lover but a lover can never be your friend." It was true in many ways. I tried hard to be a friend for her, but failed. Finally, we stopped talking again, but this time I was feeling better. This time we stopped talking for her own good. I can be proud of my decision and I was sure that even Anjana would be. I never informed Anjana of this happening, as she would start worrying about Shreya, and I wanted to prove to her that I could manage without screwing things up.

TO THE BEACHES!!!

This year my exams went great, I cleared all my lagging papers and I was on the track again. This was supposed to be my last year in the college. It has been an eventful three years. We decided to go for a trip to somewhere far, a sort of a weeklong trip. We had to bunk our classes in order to do that. That was not a big deal as we had expertise in it in the past three years. We do come up with weirdest of leave applications. It was our final year, so it was easy to fool them. We told we had an interview to attend in some place in the north and the professors happily agreed. They might have felt that finally after three years these students were doing something right. Finally, we came to a conclusion that we would travel to Goa; spend sometime at the beaches of Goa. One thing that prompted us to select Goa was the wide range of alcohol and pubs there, alcohol at the price of water, just what we were looking for. We did our reservation at one of the finest beachside resorts and also booked a car for rent. That one week was as wild as it could get. As one can say "what happens in Goa stays in Goa." We spent time in the beaches drinking beer and then back in the resort pool drinking Bacardi. It was alcohol all the way. Tried our hand in pubs and casinos but it was really not our cup of tea. We could rather spend that money on alcohol. It was a heaven for the drunks. That was probably my last trip with my friends in college and it did happen to be. I almost did everything I wanted to. Wanted to talk to Shreya for one last time and I did it. I tried to change myself and I succeeded to an extend. The one thing that was left was Neha. I had to talk to her. I knew I couldn't but it was just there in my mind as a dream. In the past three years, the relation between the two of us has widened. I had never spoken to her after that "hai". But misunderstandings and hatred increased from both the sides, but I had some special feelings for her somewhere in me. I think my so called friend Karthik had a big role to play in this, but I don't blame him. I had my chances and I let it go. I always thought of telling this to Anjana but I didn't have the strength to do so. What would she think of me?? It's not the first time I was in love or was I?? I have never felt the same about anyone. I always thought that one day she would be mine. Mine forever!!!

LAST DAYS . . . .

I gathered all my strength to talk to Neha on the last day of our college. I had to do it this day or it was never going to happen. I said bye to Anjana, she had tears in her eyes when we were leaving. She never agreed to that, she had but she knew the truth. I was to meet her the day before she left for home but I couldn't make it. I wanted to, but I didn't. Once again I failed her. I was not worth her friendship. She asked me for so little and I couldn't. Neha was over crowded by people all around her, wishing her good luck for the future. I went up to her and walked past her.

I just turned cold at that moment, I really couldn't do it. I had one last chance and I screwed things up. She was expecting me to talk to her. Four years together in the same college and all I could manage was a "Hai". The more you love a person, the greater the fear of loosing him/her. It was probably the fear of rejection that prompted me not to express myself to her. I really couldn't afford to take no as an answer. At least now, I can move out with a feeling that if I had expressed myself, she would have probably said yes. So finally the last days of college were finally over. Everything was over. No more bunking, no more ragging and no late night partying with friends. I would miss that a lot. We had a crazy party on my last day in Coimbatore, it was an emotional moment and on top of that the alcohol helped the cause. I hated that construction yard so much, but now I feel bad thinking about the fact that I can never go back there again. Can no more sit on the last bench and sleep and, most importantly, see Neha. There is a time for everything; fate has things written for all of us. A time would come when I get my true love, a time for love!!!!

LIFE AFTER COLLEGE

End of college days bring in mixed feelings in one's mind. Somewhere we are happy that we are engineers now, writing thousands of tests and exams which include the taste of failures and success. But in the end, it all comes down to one sheet of paper on which some random guy authorizes the fact that I am an engineer now. Only I know the fact as to how I got through the menace. And if majority of engineers in the country are like me, then this country is in deep shit. Whatever may be it, the fact is I survived and in this world it's all about survival and adapting to the circumstances and I did fairly well in both. But problems don't end here; it's just a beginning, as I am an engineer now, people expect me to get a job. But how can I tell those people that I never wanted to be an engineer in the first place. I am meant for something different and the fact is that I still don't know what that different thing is. I always believed that I was a very good coordinator, a team leader. I should always pursue something in that area. I started researching stuffs in my area of interest and trying to find a proper job for me before the pressure from the society gets the better off me. The usual trouble comes from your neighbours who are more interested about things going on your family, rather than setting their life right. They show as if how bothered they are about you getting a job, but in reality, they just want to go on commenting about your status of unemployment and have a good chat with their friends over tea.

In the mean time I was back in my home town of Ahmadabad. I was really missing this place and my friends round here. I never had many friends around, a small bunch, but a good one. But right now, I am jobless and most importantly, directionless. This was when I thought of studying further, but this time in something I am interested in, some courses that could enhance my leadership qualities. I wrote all the required eligibility tests and exams required for that. Meantime, I had a visit to Goa with my friends Kush and Manav, both my childhood friends. They were my partners in crime for all the deep shit that we were in during our school days. There was nothing that special about the trip except it gave some signs of something that was going to turn my life upside down. A day before we left Goa, I saw Kush sitting in our resort bedroom and talking to one of his colleagues over the phone. I never cared much about his friends and his usual chat over the phone with girls. He was always well known for that. It's strange that I am always surrounded by one such guy in my life, at first it was Gaurav and now it's Kush.

But Kush was different; he could never go past the phone calls. I never knew why, he used to say that he was least interested and I used to presume that the girls were least interested. In one such case, my assumption came true. I just came near the bed and was looking for some stuff when Kush turned and said that Anisha was saying that my voice is really husky. I didn't know what to say at that moment as I couldn't make out whether she was praising me or criticizing, because I had no clue then that girls liked husky voice. I didn't even know what the actual meaning of husky was. No one had ever praised that quality in me till then. I just said "ok" and left the room. After a while, I went to Kush and asked him what exactly she meant when she said husky. That was when I realized it was an appreciation. Then Kush gave me a background about Anisha and told me about how he liked her since the days of flying club, and even she was a trainee pilot from the same academy. We saw her picture in Facebook and just left the matter there as I wasn't interested in his love affair as she was already in a relationship. The fact was that even I lost interest in discussing about the matter, as she was in a relationship. That might be the reason why I never found her pictures that attractive at all.

Our next meeting was during Kush's birthday, he called two of his female colleagues for lunch and he asked me to join him with them. I was very hesitant about joining them, as I didn't know them and I didn't want to sit there as a fool in between their discussions. But still I went there. I was destined to go there. As it is said, "There are winds of destiny that blow when we least expect them. Sometimes they gust with the fury of a hurricane; sometimes they barely fan one's cheek. But the winds cannot be denied, bringing as they often do a future that is impossible to ignore."

When I got off my car and started walking towards the restaurant, I could see a girl waiting there on her bike with her face covered with scarf which resembled a terrorist or a Maoist. But once she removed that scarf, my heart beat slowed down, every minute details of her were getting registered in my mind, and as if my brain had slowed down the world. I still haven't lost my skills of careful examination which I developed during my college days.

What makes a woman beautiful? Is it her good looks, radiant skin, dazzling white teeth, stylish dress or her size to perfect figure? These attributes, at first glance, will surely draw most people's attention to a woman. The question is, will that first impression prove to be a facade or is there a richer beauty hidden beneath the surface?

I was one of the lucky ones to have had witnessed both the outer and the richer beauty hidden beneath the surface. She was truly a princess. I still don't know who named her that. Some one in her family had realized this beauty on the very first glance at her. Her characteristics resembled a life threatening drug, every time you look into her eyes you get more and more addicted to them and this drug has no cure and rehabilitation. If personality is an unbroken series of successful gestures, then there was something gorgeous about her, some heightened sensitivity to the promises of life, as if she were related to one of those intricate machines that register earthquakes ten thousand miles away. It was an extraordinary gift for hope, a romantic readiness such as I have never found in another person and which is unlikely that I shall ever find it again.

This is a young woman in her early twenties, who stands with an air of carefree confidence that is most noticeable in her serene eyes, outlined with a dash of kohl. Soft face with rounded cheek bones, proportionally cute nose, high trimmed brows, soft pouty pink lips, and rounded chin is complimented by her easy, charming smile. Wondrous oceans of blue gaze out in playful curiosity as she smiles; though, there is a hint of a wild spark lingering behind those lids. Dark lusty hair, groomed and shining brilliantly, which crops her gentle face; the mane glimmers down towards her shoulders, with perfectly cut tips. The uniform hair spills down between her shoulder blades in bladed formation, the rest of it cropping in circular fashion towards her shoulders where the shortest strands cover her ever sensible neck. This young woman has a soft neck and narrow shoulders that form into equally lithe arms and hands, but her midsection shouldn't go without notice. Overall, her general shape is a toned, hourglass figure defining her chest and hips which are of moderate, if not winding 'definition'. Altogether her skin tone is a light & even tan lending her to porcelain glamour. She is a feathery woman, but owns too many womanly curves that are upheld with firm seductive looks.

It takes a lot to provoke such interest from me, really. Normally, I tend to write about scenery, emotional ploys. In this case, she was a rare exception. There are also paintings that have provided me enough reason to write, but when it comes down to it, most of my inspiration comes from the inside. There was just something unreal and eerie about her. Her luminous face adds an extra tone to it. The eyes were piercingly sharp, which spoke a thousand words with a blink. Plump, the lips had the strangest curl to them. Overall, she was truly an unearthly beauty.

The birthday party went excellent and I hardly spoke or noticed the birthday boy. But I would always be thankful to Kush for compelling me to attend the party. But I really didn't understand what I was doing. I liked a girl in a relationship and who is also being liked by one of my close friends. I could sense that things were going to get ugly sooner or later. But all those hindrances or obstacles were not bothering me at the moment. I felt that there was no need to run my thoughts this wild, as I was just appreciating her. I was never expecting to meet or talk to her ever again.

BREAKTHROUGH AUSTRALIAN TRIP

In the coming days, Kush was very busy with his preparations to go to Australia for training. He was getting an opportunity to train on a multi engine plane in Australia. This gave rise to a complete change in Kush's English accent. He tends to do that quite often; I think he was trying to get a feel of Australia. But frankly I hate this fake accent by people. People try to fake accent once they land on a foreign soil. I never gave a shit about his accent or his new makeover. I met him a day before he left for Australia to wish him for his training. That was when I heard about Anisha next. He said, he had given my number to Anisha, if she wanted to know anything or needed any help in his absence. I just nodded and changed the topic, because I was sure she would never call up to inquire and all.

But in this instance, I was lucky to be wrong, she did call up. It is really funny about my friends and the friendship we have. We never used to care much about each other. It was so natural for us. For instance, I never remembered any of my friend's birthday, the only way I used to come to know was through Facebook updates and I made sure to write it on his wall just as a formality. But I always expected and made sure that we looted the guy in the name of birthday treat. I am not the only jerk in this; all my friends were equally bad at this. But to some extent it changed when I was in college. Birthdays would be like a huge carnival, we have preparations and surprise parties for the birthday boy and we make sure that we get a good gift for him and then in return he treats us. But back in Ahmadabad, things haven't changed much, it's been 48 hrs since Kush left and I didn't even thought once whether he reached his destination safely. I just completely forgot about it until I received a call from the unexpected. Yup, it was Anisha. She seemed bit worried and asked me whether I received any call from Kush that is when I realized that Kush was in Australia. But I acted smart then, I didn't want her to have a bad impression about me or our friendship. I jumped on to say that even I was expecting his call for long and would let her know if I got any call from him. I even asked her to do the same if he called her. I expected Kush to call her for obvious reasons.

Kush did call us both the next day. And as promised I informed her about the same. Even she told that she was about to call me to inform the same. We then chatted for a while, and then got back to our respective work. It was always different talking to her. The only way to explain it is that it brought a smile on my face. I used to feel pleasant and happy after talking to her. The pleasant and happy feelings continued in the coming months as we used to talk a lot on the phone and meet too. We found many similarities in each other's character and behaviour and, most importantly, we understood each other's problems. We started discussing anything and everything with each other. We became very good friends with time. But that is when we faced with our first hurdle, Kush. By the time Kush came back from his training in Australia, we were like the best of friends. We never realized the fact that, importance of one another had increased far beyond what Kush could imagine, and had taken a place above Kush in our lives. This never went well with Kush; this was the beginning of distances between Kush and the two of us. Kush could never accept the fact that I and Anisha were more close to each other than he ever was. It further increased on New Year's Eve. Kush hosted a party at his place on New Year's Eve. I was in the invitee list, which also included Anisha and her friend Disha. Disha happens to be her childhood friend and they always celebrate new years together. I, along with Kush, went that day to pick Anisha from her place. We went in my love machine. I think I haven't introduced anyone to my love machine, that's my first car. The name given to the car would be justified soon, as it has witnessed some of the beautiful moments in my life. But for now, I would stick to me picking them up from their home. Roads were jam packed as expected. It took us more than an hour to travel this 10 km ride from Kush's home to Anisha's. The most stunning thing about the day was, no doubt, Anisha. Even today she remembers the expression that I gave back then. It was something out of this world. While Kush had gone to her house to call her, I was waiting near the car, as I received some phone call. It was usual on that day as it was New Year's Eve. As Anisha walked out, her sparkling eyes in the moonlight and her gorgeous hair covering up her face sideways, it was deadly. I never realized that my mouth was wide open. I had always seen this scene in a Bollywood movie but never believed in something like that till then. But believe me, it did happen that day and thankfully, the only person who saw that was Anisha. I think those deadly looks were the trigger to what followed in future. Suddenly I had feelings for one of my closest friend. I knew it was not right but I couldn't help it. "There is never a time or place for true love. It happens accidentally, in a heartbeat, in a single flashing, throbbing moment." And I believe that was my moment. We drove and all of us got to our party venue before 12. We thought of watching a movie at first with some scotch for the guys and vodka for the ladies. As always I and Anisha loved each other's company, we were watching movie together. We usually used to ignore our surroundings and it would seem as if we were alone in each other's company. Disha being Anisha's close friend could sense that there was something more to it, which we both forcefully denied. I still don't remember the movie, neither does Anisha. I believe none in the party remembers the movie as me and Anisha were busy talking to each other, and the others were busy staring at us. All this didn't go that well with Kush, as it was his party and it was meant to impress Anisha. He tried now and then to gather her attention and put light to the effort he had made in coming up with this party. He made arrangements for the finest scotch and vodka in a region where alcohol is prohibited. He really meant business with the party and I did screw it up for his big time. Kush stopped the movie in between, as it became obvious by now that no one was interested in it anyway. He came up with another strategy that was to play something interactive, so that he could get to know about her more. So we started playing the drinking game. I never realized by this time that I was a bit drunk and Anisha was no less. We were so lost in our talks that we never realized how much we drank. This led to a series of things that happened and we never realized it. At least I didn't realize it . . . .

NEW YEAR KISS

As midnight marched through the worlds time zones, it was the start of a new year, ushering out the old and toasting the new. The same high spirited celebrations were going on at Kush's place too. We all greeted the New Year with hugs and wishes, the first of which I received from Anisha. I still don't understand what it was. The hug just went on for ages. It might be just my belief or did we just hug for a usually long period. Whatever the moment was, it was interrupted by a series of phone calls on both the sides from friends and relatives. When I was done with all my phone calls, I turned towards Anisha and I found her still busy with different calls she was getting. But the most shocking and unusual thing about all this was that we were holding hands when all this was going on. To be very clear, it was very difficult to dial numbers and find contacts from your phone book, with one hand, but I never noticed any such difficulties. I was still lost in the New Year hug. After all our phone calls, we went back to our usual conversation and some drinking game. We started this game in Kush's room as his parents were going to sleep by then. After a while, we all thought of taking a nap, by this time we all were totally drunk. This time, Anisha was holding my head and I was leaning over her, as I couldn't sit erect for a minute with all this alcohol in my body. It was becoming too heavy for me to do so. I don't exactly remember when we decided to sleep but we did. We all just slept near his bed. Anisha was sleeping next to me and Kush and others followed after that on the lower side of the bed. It took me no time to sleep as alcohol was really helping the cause. The next I remember is that I was in my dreams. This was one of my rare dreams which I still remember and there are obvious reasons behind it. I felt a foggy picture of a woman dressed in black lying next to me. We were sleeping quite close to each other. I was quick to identify that it was Anisha. The mixture of her perfume and body lotion had a seductive touch in the air. After a while, I realized I was sleeping with my hands over her and we felt comfortable as it helped us to beat the cold. All those instances come to my mind as small fragments. It was really a weird dream as it was never continuous. The complete scenario was broken down into small fragments. The next and the last scene I remember was when we kissed. The moment was priceless and care free. I never thought once as to what I was doing and how I could do it. It was my dream and I am not answerable to anyone. Then the next fragment, I heard noise from round Anisha and saw her wake up, I opened my eyes to find out that others had woken up and Kush was ready to drop Anisha and her friend back home. I could sense that Kush was not happy with the proceedings yesterday, as I stole all the limelight and attention and his efforts went unnoticed. Kush had to drop them back as I still had a bad hangover from last night. I thought of going back to my place and started walking downstairs with them. Suddenly, Anisha turned back and went back to the room. That was when I saw her face for the first time that morning. Her face suggested that she wanted me to follow her to the room, as if she wanted to tell something to me. But I was too sleepy to respond to any such facial expressions. We waited for her downstairs for sometime and then left for our respective places once she was back. I was alone while driving back home, suddenly I saw a message on my phone. I was literally taken aback by the message. It stated that Anisha doesn't want to talk to me from now on and not to contact her ever. I really couldn't understand what was going on. Everything was going so well and suddenly such a message was hard to digest. I made my way back home as fast as I could and called her up. She refused to take my call at first but then made herself available at my request. Then she explained things to me that I could never have accepted, if it was told by someone else. She made me realize that all the things I presumed to be a dream was nowhere near a dream and it actually took place last night. I felt disgusted and ashamed at the same time. I was literally speechless but gathered strength to convince her that I never did any of that in purpose. I convinced her to meet me sometime so that I could get an opportunity to prove my innocence. I quickly took bath, made some lame excuses to my mother, and left to see Anisha . . . .

I still, even today, think of what happened that night, the incident that changed both our lives for ever. In some way, it was good, as it was a true test of our bond and relation that we shared with people around us. It was the time for them to stand by us. The incident helped us identify our true loved ones.

I always used to ridicule Bollywood movie scenes, when we saw such affairs on screen, and we used to call the actors names. But that incident made us both think and find out why it had happened. I had to come up with some justification to convince myself first, before I could convince Anisha of this. Even Anisha had no clue as to how things went wrong in her simple and straight forward life. I understood a peculiar thing about our subconscious mind, which in my case was the culprit behind this situation. Our subconscious can't process negatives. It interprets everything we think as a positive thought. So if I think, 'I don't want to be poor,' our unconscious mind focuses on the "poor" and, because it doesn't do negatives, the thought becomes 'I want to be poor.' Being poor then becomes the goal in your subconscious mind and like a young child, desperate to please, it helps you behave in a way that will keep you poor, obviously not what you wanted. The same thing happened in our case. I, on one side, was always fond of Anisha. She was the type of person I always wanted to end up with, but on knowing her relationship status I always told myself that I could not love her and it was not morally right. I think, my dumb brain, on the other side, processed it as, "I can love her as it is morally right". Many would find this as a stupid reasoning to justify my doings, but I have no intention of doing so. I know what happened was wrong, but it was unintentional. But in Anisha's case a different situation played an important role. There were various incidents in the few months before the new year that were pretty disturbing for Anisha. She was already struggling to keep up to the disappointments she was facing professionally, and the one person she wanted there to be with her then, was constantly indulging in fights with her. The only support she found was in her friend, that's me. All the incidents, in which I ended up supporting her, were collected and stored in her subconscious mind. Her Subconscious mind already had a picture of a person who should be her soul mate. That picture had a face in the form of her boy friend, but most of the qualities of that picture were fulfilled by me, and she expected the same in her boyfriend. This mix up of characters in your mind disturbs you like anything. This makes it difficult for us to understand and realize what exactly we feel for that person. Was it affection or love? There is a lot of difference between the two which many fail to understand and result in misunderstanding their true loved ones. A person can get attracted towards two people at the same time. Or subconsciously a person might think that if the person he or she is with right now is not there in the future, the other person can fill the gap. Here, the fear psychosis plays a major role. So in this case who's created the fear psychosis? There should be someone to blame in this case. Anisha cannot be blamed completely for the incident. Me, along with her boyfriend, has equal role to play in the incidents that led to this situation. Her boyfriend never gave the trust or the feeling of security, she was always asking for. She was not the type of person interested in casual relationship. She wanted her first love to be the last and everlasting one. But who knows her boyfriend had other plans or did he have any plans at all?? He himself used to emphasize the fact that he had no clue of the future. This was the beginning of the fear psychosis that took up most of her subconscious mind and she saw another person who was willing to fill in that gap. How can a girl be blamed for that? Somewhere or the other I believe every girl would agree to my findings. Security and time is the most important things in a female's life. That stands true of all social animals around us.

This is tough on the part of an individual. How often do we find true love in the first place? And how frustrating it is when we find it, but it comes at such an inopportune time, such as when we are in another relationship! Of course it's ideal if we can leave the current relationship for a shot at a new one, but it's not always that easy. Sometimes you can't leave, or other times we don't want to leave, in which case we try to balance both the relationships. But can we really do this and keep everyone happy?

Another function of the unconscious mind is to present repressed memories in order to release trapped emotions. So when our mind is filled with all this junk and thousands of unanswered questions, shit happens. But things get out of hand when the factor of morality plays its role. The subconscious mind will keep us on the straight and narrow path of whatever morality it has learned, by enforcing its morality on us, even if society judges that morality wrong. A terrorist will kill and destroy without qualms, because his moral code teaches him that he is a freedom fighter. But that doesn't justify his actions. So if your subconscious decides that you deserve to be punished, then you will be wracked with guilt and exhibit behaviours designed to punish yourself, even though there are no laws to say that what your subconscious mind sees as bad, is actually so.

We all make personal, financial and business decisions, confident that we have properly weighed all the important factors and acted accordingly—and that we know how we came to those decisions. But since we know only our conscious influences, we have only partial information. As a result, our view of ourselves and our motivations, and of society, is like a jigsaw puzzle with most of the pieces missing. We fill in blanks and make guesses, but the truth about us is far more complex and subtle than that which can be understood as the straightforward calculation of conscious and rational minds. We perceive, we remember our experiences, we make judgments, we act and in all of these endeavours we are influenced by factors that we aren't aware of. The truth is that one's subconscious mind is active, purposeful, and independent. Hidden, its intentions may be, but their effects are anything but hidden, for they play a critical role in shaping the way our conscious mind experiences and responds to the world.

These intense researches were done so as to keep myself away from the so called path of guilt and make sure that Anisha did the same. It's always easy for a guy to escape from such incidents, as our culture and society have been so designed. If such incidents take place, a guy's friends would praise him for being such a stud and the girl's friend would point fingers at her for being a slut. When we talk of equality, both parties should be treated with the same respect. So, I had to prove everyone that what happened was nowhere a slutty incident, and wanted to protect Anisha from the blame game that was going to follow soon. A test of our morals and the friendship we share . . . .

ANISHA

The need to be loved is exceptionally strong in all human beings. From childhood to old age, humans want to be loved by those around them. Love connects people in the strongest of ways. It produces care and concern, without which no one would take the responsibility of looking after others. Love makes the difficulties of life bearable, and helps ease the struggles of life. Life cannot just run on cold and hard rules. The warmth of love is necessary to infuse spirit and joy in life. A home without love, however orderly and organized, cannot fulfil its true purpose. A family is not just a micro-organization where the needs of members are met. A family's outstanding characteristic is that, members love one another, and this emotion binds them together.

I believe that I am somehow out of this equation of love, when it comes to my family at least that is what

I used to feel. I would never say that my parents were not loving enough or caring enough. They actually were very dedicated and caring, the result of which could be seen in the type of education and lifestyle that my parents provided me. My father made sure that I was sent to the best school and had the best lifestyle which was, back then, difficult for a government employee, who had the responsibility of a big family to run. They were just not expressive enough. This need for expression took me for a horrific nightmare which I regret till date.

I feel my perception of love and affection didn't match their way of expression. I wanted my parents to let me know that they loved me. At this mature age, when I look back, the way my family treated and disciplined me, it was great. But for a child, in her early teen, I wanted people to express their love, everything else that one does around her, is purely materialistic. I wanted people's time and understanding, which, I feel, I never got. This led to a strong bond, I formed with a few. Those few still hold an important place in my heart. One friend among them held a much higher position of them all, and that was Rohan who would be my first true love and to whom I gave everything. I would say that, I fell in love with a person even before I started loving myself. I had never pampered myself or loved myself till then. I was proud of my cold and tomboy kind of behaviour. I was never known for my girly trends and attitudes.

I would have never imagined that I would be taken for a roller coaster ride when I first met Anurag. A person who showed me what was missing in my life and brought a sense of wanting for acceptance in me.

He seemed to be a simple, down to earth, guy who was really silent and very much attached to his family. Even months before meeting him, I had heard a lot about him through one of my friends, Kush. So I had a preconceived image of Anurag which was of a good hearted young guy. I would say he was more or less the same as my premonition suggested. After knowing each other through Kush, we finally met at Kush's birthday party. We actually didn't leave any impression; we just had a quite get together before Kush was going abroad for his training. I shared a good bond with Kush then, he was one of the few friends I had from the academy. This is how our friendship began, it started through Kush and within a few meetings we formed some kind of unexplainable bond which later by passed Kush from the picture.

Somewhere down the line, Anurag made me realize that I was not respecting myself enough. From what he had known about me from my explanations, I was an independent and bold person, at least I tried to show it that way in public. I started believing and trusting his words, actually what he was saying was true, but when one looks back at those days, it wasn't that bad after all. I was happy with the new found love in my life in the form of Rohan.

The incidents to follow broke me and my relationship with Rohan. I learned it the hard way that this immaturity, both of experience and emotion, can cause one to think they are in love when they are in fact infatuated. This infatuation can cause one to experience low self-esteem, devastation and depression when the relationship comes to a sudden end. I would never call that a three year relationship infatuation. I still believe

that it was true love for me but was it the same for him?
I can never prove that anymore. If the incident between
me and Anurag wouldn't have happened that day then
Rohan would have got a chance to prove his love to me
through a long term commitment which he was phobic
about. He always had this "But" in his sentence which
made me really handicapped. This insecurity from his
side was the main reason for me to get swayed for the
first and last time in my life. It's a female trend in all
beings, whether social or non social. Females tend to
give security a priority, let that be career, love or even
one's day to day routine.

Break up with Rohan was a trauma but Anurag
was there besides me as he shared equal blame for the
incident and accepted that. With time, I regained
myself and that too in a strong and bold manner.
Having such a strong relationship at such a young age
was an experience that has taught me, for the better
rather than the worse. Having those feelings taught
me that you have to consider other people and also
to stand up for yourself. The knowledge I now have
of how someone can treat me and why someone may
say certain things to me, has matured me in such a
way that I never thought possible. The lesson of love,
I learned, is knowledge that I can pass on. So I now
think of it as an experience and thrive on the knowledge
now, rather than depress myself. He did console me
through encouraging words like; it is not as if I've done
something against the law. I had fallen for a guy who
might not have the respect that I deserve and which I
earned through three years of at most dedication and
commitment.

I somehow feel that this boldness had a huge role to play in my future relationships. I still need to find a balance between the cold and soft side of mine. I am still part of a learning curve deciding as to whom to trust and to what extent and at what time.

It is always hard to be practical, when you are in love. This was the same complexity that happened in my life too. I always knew that Rohan had many online friends whom he used to chat with, and many of them had a crush and liking towards him. He used to be very secretive about his personal life, whereas I was an open book in front of him. The insecurity grew as I always expected in return whatever I was providing him with, whether it was information, commitment or love. All my doubts were proved right, once we broke up as he went on to be in a relationship with an online friend, he earlier had. I would never be able to prove whether he knew her even when we were seeing each other.

ANJANA

Things began to change after college. Everyone expect it to change but it was quick and drastic. We both got busy with our own work and Anurag was planning to go to France for his studies. We both stopped texting and slowly communication between us stopped for a certain period of time. But there was always one appreciable thing about him, that he made sure to let me know whenever there was something important going on in his life. It made me happy as, irrespective of the distance and lack of communication, he still considered me his best friend. But I never did the same; I stopped sharing my stuffs, once I moved to Bangalore. I was so lost and involved in my work that I didn't have time to socialize and catch up with old days.

When he first told about Anisha, I never even listened to it completely. I thought it would be the same as your old relationship. It would be just an infatuation and a few days of namesake relationship. I still knew Anurag as the one in college, but never realized as to how much he had changed and evolved from then. There were reasons for me not trusting him in the matter of relationships, not one but many. His past would play an important part and above that he was leaving for France in a few weeks. I couldn't see him handling relationships in general and now we were talking about distant ones. But Anurag surprised me; he did keep up with the relationship even after going abroad. He did put in his everything and the amount of dedication was commendable. I was able to see a new Anurag who respected others' feelings and the influence of Anisha was evident from his interaction even towards us. Only I knew the reason for the change in him, others among his school friends could only wonder.

MY LOVE MACHINE

I tried my max to be with her during this traumatic phase of hers. I had never seen Anisha in such a terrible state of mind. I could never even think of leaving her alone for one bit as no one could predict what she would end up doing otherwise. I could not physically be by her side, I was in France, but I made sure that the VoIP service provided ended up in profit that year because of my 24*7 usage of the their service. I literally used to do my part time jobs just to be able to do a VoIP recharge everyday, but I made sure that I would be there for her whenever she felt lonely. Somewhere I believed that I was the main accused for her break up and this state of her. The Anisha everyone knew was so lively and fun loving and the one they were seeing was dull and lost. I believed, I had a major role to play in that. The male chauvinist side of me never believed that I alone was to blame for the happening, as I never forced anyone into any relationship. I just expressed myself as I didn't want to do the same mistake which I did in the case of Neha, but keeping all those fights and confusions to myself, I was with her in all the turmoils of life.

All the problems in her personal and professional life, brought us close. She used to share everything and anything with me and we formed a certain level of magical bond between us. We started reliving the moments which we once thought were taboo but now as time passed by; we started ignoring the logic out of the moment, and just thought of it on the emotional front. She knew it that I still loved her, but after the bumpy start we got; she was not ready to accept the love. I always used to tell her that she had taken me for granted and would realize the value of my presence once I was not there. I came back to India for my semester break and a time came when we got to test our relationship and perhaps name it. I had to leave for my ancestral place for a marriage and I was so busy there that I could not manage the same frequency of calls which we both were used to. This absence from her life just brought out the love in her for me which she was pressing in for quite long.

We thought of meeting up after a long gap and quite a few hours of telephonic conversations. The last time we met in person, it led to her break up and the disasters that followed. But this time our meetings and what happened during our meetings were no accidents. It was just the expression of feelings that we had for each other and we didn't have to regret any of those. Most of the times our meetings were in my car as we were not allowed to meet in public, because of our so called taboo, which made us name our car the love machine. This was the car, which started the love between the two of us and it was the apt name which we could give to the car. I used to make a hundred reasons to get out of the office before time so that I could spend more time with Anisha. We loved each other's company, we still didn't accept that we were in a relationship, but we actually didn't care to name it, at least she didn't. She was the one who used to question me about it, but always ran away from the answer, never knew why. This question haunted me forever as I always ended up on the insecure side of it.

ANISHA

Anurag was my support system during my days of isolation and trauma. I had distanced myself from most of my dear friends and in a few cases they had distanced from me. I used to spend most of the time talking to Anurag on the phone; he used to take the pain to call me up everyday from France. I slowly found comfort in his presence, it might be because of my state of mind or it might be true love, I don't know that yet.

We used to talk all the time and were happy in each other's company, just the two of us. Anurag met me when he came to India for his holidays, we had a good time chatting. He always made me feel special with all his gifts and pampering, I started feeling that this was what I always wanted. I wanted someone to treat me as a princess and pamper and spoil me to the core. We sometimes had some cosy and romantic moments of our own, but we were not ready to name our relationship, we were stern on believing that we were just friends. Anurag used to tease me that I would start loving him only when he left me. That's just what happened; he didn't leave in actual terms but went to his hometown for a marriage. He was very busy those days that he didn't have the time to talk to me, at the same magnitude at which we used to. This really made me restless and lonely most of the time. I don't want to accept, but it was true that I was in love with Anurag or least to say, I could not live within his absence. I was so used to him there by my side, that absence for a few days was making me go mad about him. He came back a week later and we thought of meeting up, I told him how badly I missed him, and he was smiling and taunting me by saying that he knew it would happen, as he had told me earlier. I didn't know what happened in between, but we ended up kissing each other in our love machine. This is what we had named his car. The name was put in after what happened this day. We kept on talking to each other while kissing and this was no accident. This was the first real non-accidental kiss we had. We broke all boundaries and restrictions; we had put on ourselves by calling ourselves so called friends. This went on for more than an hour, we never realized how fast the time passed by. I could see Anurag cursing the time, as it was really late at night and it was time for him to drop me back home and head back himself. Even I didn't want to leave. I wanted to just break free of all the shackles that I had put on myself because of my own feelings and the reactions of people around me.

We had this love machine meeting on a regular basis till Anurag went back to France. In between that, Anurag introduced me to his family and we even had good times at his home, I mean the love machine kind of good times. We used to go out, mostly to the city outskirts as we couldn't risk meeting each other in public, as friends might come to know about us. We even used to make these meetings at our houses, when the surroundings and situation were apt. I also used to see him at his office after office hours and we used to go back home together. I never asked him much about his business, as I didn't know anything outside my profession, so no use asking something which I was least interested in or had knowledge in. I was a regular invitee during all his family occasions and festivals. It was all going smooth except a certain tumour that was growing in our relationship, which rather went unnoticed or to say we ignored it on purpose.

I never revealed our relationship in public or to my friends, whereas it was not the case with Anurag. He introduced me to most of his friends, one by one, and even I was in good contact with most of them. But I always hesitated, as my friends would never accept him as they believed that Anurag was the reason behind bringing my three year long relation down to rubbles. I would never blame Anurag alone; I had equal part to play in it. I should have never supported the feelings he had for me.

This was the start of cracks forming in our relationship. The very thought that I was with a guy who was the reason behind my break up, tormented me a lot, this didn't go well with me at all. By this time, I was selected to the academy and Anurag had a huge role in motivating me and helping me with all the interviews. He was getting more and more into me by every passing day, whereas I was beginning to move away from him. The academy made things worse, as I was so busy with my work and I found solace in a group of friends I found in the academy. We formed a bond from the punishments that we used to get together. I even had a soft corner towards a certain person in the academy. We were not allowed phones, so I hardly had any contacts with Anurag. He used to send regular letters and they were really sweet. I was really moved by the birthday gift that he once sent me. I still carry them with me, but I was really not able to consider him my love, because of all the odds that I saw in front of me or the odds that perhaps I created on my own.

ANURAG

I often wonder whether things actually had to end like this. Could there have been an alternative, was I being too arrogant at times? But as soon as these thoughts start eating me out with guilt, I start thinking of all that she had done to me, the way I was treated by her. She used to act really selfish at times. It might be the same with any person in that situation, but I am not here to justify her actions. On one side, she wanted me to move on in life and when I started thinking on those lines, she started giving me hopes of things working out between the two of us. I have often heard quotes and sayings talking about a woman's mind. "It is hard to understand them" and "it is impossible to know what they are thinking" and blah blah blah!! Never knew that the level of difficulty would be this high. It is as if what ever we think or assume is going to be proved wrong and they make it such that it is our mistake that we are not able to understand them. It is not because they are complex; it's just that we are not efficient enough to match their intellect.

My life stands as a clear example as to how pathetic one's relationship can go. If we draw a graph of it, it would easily resemble a product life cycle and now it is in the region of decline. The complete product in this case my relationship was a failure, neither its rise was as expected, neither the maturity and nor is the decline. A very good example of a very bad product it is. She often used to say that she got lost when she was busy. She doesn't get time for anything. She gets really cold at times. The fact was that I have never seen her like that. She was a struggling talented pilot at the time I saw her, who was willing to work hard to achieve her goals. At least that was how she portrayed herself in front of me. It is funny that now I have started having two meanings to all her quotes, first is the one which she tries to convey and the second is the one which I perceive.

The first few days, after she joined the training academy, were bit weird. In these two years of knowing each other, never had I seen a day without her phone call or at least a message to whish me good morning or goodnight. It used to happen that my day used to start seeing her message in my inbox, which brought a smile to my face, and so I used to believe that I would have a rocking day ahead of me. She used to be my lucky charm and so I used to consult her before taking any decision in my life. Even the smallest actions needed her opinion. It used to just ooze in confidence within me. I was always sure of success, as I was literally over confident on her confidence. Even though I do not believe in idol worship, I was actually a bit superstitious about these matters. And when it comes to these matters, she was no less. That was something common in us during our early days; we used to hate certain odd numbers to such an extent that we never even kept the volume of our car music system on those numbers. We even didn't listen to songs on such numbers even if it turned out to be the chartbuster of the year.

My life was really empty, once she got a job, that was when I realized that how isolated I was in my friends circle after getting in to a relationship with her. I was so into her that I never took out time for any other friends or occasion. This didn't help me at this moment as I really found myself lonely. I was not even allowed to call her, as phones were not allowed at her place. She would get an opportunity to call from a public telephone at her canteen at a particular time of the day. And if by coincidence, I was busy with some other work at that time or if I didn't hear the phone ring, then I would have to again wait for a whole week for her call and also repent over the fact that I was unable to pick the call last time around. I really felt very strong about our relationship as we were actually putting in some effort to make it work or was it just me putting all the effort and I was assuming that she was doing the same. I was somehow living in a dream world and was ready to believe only the positive sides of what was happening, as if I was so determined to make it a happy ending story. This sometimes made me ignore certain facts that were totally against my dream end.

This was one of the worst times in my life with respect to finances. I was in a very bad financial crunch. If I didn't work for a month, then I could turn bankrupt, my bank account was going in such a delicate state. This led to my journey to the south of France, a city called Lyon, the city known for its young crowd and party atmosphere. But that was not what took me to Lyon. It was a part time job that one of my friends arranged. This was in between my tight thesis schedule. But I did not have any option as I had been sitting idle for quite a few months, leading to this financial crunch of mine. Those few weeks of my life were a time when I mingled more out with my friends in France. I really had a lot of time to socialize, as most of my daily routine was taken up by Skype calls and VoIP calls with Anisha. I still couldn't believe that during my first six months of stay in France, I spent almost fifteen thousand on phone calls with her. If I could manage a bit more, I could have brought Anisha to France. The most difficult thing out here was that Anisha used to get time to call me in the evenings on Sundays, whereas I would be at work at the same time and we were not allowed to take up calls during the period. It was money vs Anisha. It was an obvious choice back then and it would be Anisha. Money was equally important at that point of time, it was a matter of my survival.

Everything was going so good, or at least I assumed it was. There was a gradual change in her behaviour. She was slowly going away from me. She had justification even for that. She used to tell me that the academy had made her numb. She was turning phobic towards this institution of love and relationships. So what was she trying to tell me? If the same sentence was to be said by a guy then this is how it would sound "I am fed up of this relationship and would like to move on in life, I have a hectic job upfront and have something to achieve in life. I really do not have time to waste on these matters." It's funny how girls can manage such a long explanation in one sentence. One cannot blame a person for being ambitious in life. Anisha was a person who aimed big in life, a typical scorpion trend, but what she was not realising was what its side effects were. Whenever you take such bold aggressive stance, you tend to hurt certain people on the way. In this case I didn't know who all these some people were but I was certainly there on the list.

I still remember how upset we used to get, when we were not able to talk to each other during the first few weeks of academy life, when I used to miss her weekend phone calls. I used to be so happy seeing her making efforts to call to France. On a financial note, I used to feel that finally my fifteen thousand is being paid off and, on the other side; I could see the effort made by her. Talking about efforts, before joining the academy she was so impressed by my love for her, she had promised me that she would be talking to her friends about me, when she returned from the academy, and make sure that they started accepting me as well. Those promises sure did take me to a dream ride for a while, but never knew about the dark clouds which were hovering above, the storm which was going to rip my dreams apart. Half way through her training sessions her weekly calls turned into once in two weeks conversation, that too for max five minutes. I used to assume that she was getting busier, as her trainings were half way through. By the time her training got over, it was just one call a month and that too strangely, all were made by me and I used to get the same excuse every time that she just received her phone and she was about to call me. I really tried hard to believe what she used to say. I genuinely did but I always had the slightest of doubt still left in my mind as to whether it was a sign of a break up. She always used to complain to me about my doubts and lack of trust in her. What else do you expect a guy like me to do? First of all, I am possessive about her, she even wants and likes some one to be possessive about her. Second of all, it was a hidden relationship; none in her circle even knew what I was to her or what exactly our relationship was. It took us almost a year to name our relationship in the first place. I was always scared as there were hundreds of guys around her trying for her. Most of them disguised as friends. She was the kind of person who gave friendship a lot of importance and there were guys who took advantage of that and ended up proposing her, not knowing that she was in a relationship, which was true in the real world. All those guys who were hiding their feelings, when she was in her first relationship, came out in the open describing their feelings for her. Even though I curse them now and then, I cannot blame them as they did not do anything wrong, they just proposed a single girl. But why didn't Anisha react the way I or any other boyfriend would want her girl friend to react. She used to explain to me how certain guy used to propose her every month and certain crushes that she used to have on some of them. I really never understood her. What was she trying to portray herself as? When I recall all these incidents, it turns out to be a calculated arrangement in which she always turns out to be on the safer side, as she was always updating me about her feelings. She was not lying to me or neither was she cheating on me. But the important question stays unanswered, does she love me anymore? It was a strange transition in which we turned to friends again. When I recall those six months, I do not understand the point at which we were friends again. Or at least we planned to act as friends. But on the other side, her going away from me was dragging me more and more into her. This led me to her academy.

BACK TO INDIA &
ACADEMY

Meanwhile, I also had something very important academically going on in my life. My thesis was round the corner. Was keeping myself busy with all the last minute submissions and meeting deadlines. I left Lyon as it was time I concentrated my complete energy on my final presentation. My final presentation was not the end of matters; I had a bigger decision to take just after my thesis. As it would be obvious that I would be a master of engineering by then, but the important decision was regarding my career, whether or not to stay in France after my studies or go back to India and search for a job there. Reason for me to stay back in France was better life, freedom, alcohol and great pay. And my reason for not staying back in France was just Anisha. This shows how bad I was in weighing stuffs and prioritizing life. On one side, there was a girl who was so focussed that she was ready to let go of anything for her career, and on the other side there was a guy who was ready to let go anything for that girl. They both were common in one aspect, they both were focused on their goals, but the bad news was that they both had goals which were poles apart.

My colloquium was set on 29th August, an auspicious day for all the mallus around the world. It was the time for Onam, a harvest festival in Kerala. It is considered to be the most important day in the lives of people in that part of the world. And it sure was an important day for me too. I had my master thesis colloquium set on that day. I was really tense for two reasons. I was wearing a suite in which I was really uncomfortable and secondly I was presenting in front of the toughest professors in the university. I was not expecting an A grade from them at all, but as a human tendency, you always have a small optimistic side of yours saying that what if I get an A.

By this time, I had started hating Anisha a bit. I did think of her, as I used to call her up on all the important days of her life. I expected the same from her but I was sure that was not going to happen. Reason was pretty simple, Anisha never knew any important stuffs going on in my life. The very thought does hurt but she never used to enquire anything about me. Whenever I used to call her, the complete conversation used to be me asking about things going on in her life, her experiences and after that me voluntarily informing about things happening in my life. I always used to crave for certain questions from her part. I do wonder whether she even knows what I do for a living. Earlier

I used to think that it's part of her character as she doesn't understand anything apart from flying. But that was not the case, even today, if you ask her what her ex does, she would let you know in detail. So what was I? For people reading this, it would be clear that I was used as a rebound but it is difficult for me to swallow the idea of rebound and that too with me. Why am I going through all this? Is it because of the things that I did to her? The only mistake I feel was that I loved her. Actually it wasn't a mistake, it just happened. No one ever thought things would end up in such a big mess. Never thought Anisha would respond to my feelings, she had never done so in the past. But whatever may be it, that one expression of my feelings has led me to this disastrous and unrecoverable state. The only thing that keeps me moving is the famous quote from Oscar Wilde, "When one is in love, one always begins by deceiving oneself, and one always ends by deceiving others. That is what the world calls a romance." I was being deceived and always kept on convincing myself of the false perception I was living in. But all this negativity just vanished in a glance when I got a call. The name on it said, "Anisha Calling". The very first noticeable difference you could find in me was a smile on my face and the other was excitement in my body language. I immediately forgot that in an hour's time I would be facing the test from my professors. I just wanted to enjoy the moment and wanted to sound as excited as possible. I received the call and she immediately wished me for onam. My excitement level decreased from a 10 to 8, still a good rating considering the presentation I was having in some time. I felt it wouldn't be difficult for her to remember Onam, as her academy was in Kerala. But still I was happy as when she thought of Onam she could relate it to me. As always I had to tell her about things going on in my life, after I inquired about her. I told her about the presentation that I was having in sometime and I would want her to wish me luck as I always considered her as my lucky charm. She brushed aside my superstitious nature and told me that I would do good as I have worked hard and all the logical shit into the discussion.

It is very obvious for an individual, especially an atheist like me that one is rewarded for the work one does. I always believed in the concept of *karma*. But every individual gets his or her confidence by certain consoling and encouraging words spoken by our loved ones. It really changes our perception towards the situation. If we consider the situation in the game of cricket, Bangladesh has never won a match of cricket against Australia, but that doesn't mean that their coach doesn't encourage them before they face them the next time. Such encouragements bring in confidence among them that they can do it. They might fail for sure, but at least those words from the coach bring within them a fighting spirit. Similarly, I know that if I want to do good, I need to work hard, I can't act like certain movies and have a lucky charm besides me to get things done. The funniest thing here is that Anisha herself believed in these small superstitions till she got into the academy. She might still be doing the same. She used to ask me to pray for her, do stuffs like parrot card reading. She used to subscribe horoscope to her mails everyday, and hearing stuffs like logic from such a person doesn't actually have any logic. But anyway, it wasn't something new for me. I wished her back for her passing out ceremony, which as usual I had remembered. This was the end of our ten minute conversation after a month long gap. After keeping the call, I realized that it was better off without her call. I wasn't realizing the fact that I was getting numb and disturbed each time she called me. My mind would be filled with a thousand doubts and questions every time she called. But, she was getting more bold and cold towards me after every call. She used to tell me about a male colleague of hers, with whom she hanged out and how people around them felt that they were in a relationship. The only thing I could manage after that was a smile and to control the flow of tears from my eyes. There are certain things, I never understand about girls. They are so sensitive when it comes to their issues, but where does all that go when they are talking about someone else. Anisha always knew about my feelings for her, but she always acted as if I was a non living thing and used to explain all those infatuations of hers with great interest to me. She used to tell me about all the gifts that she got from certain guys and how things went with them. I hadn't seen one instance when she said the same about the gifts given by me. Ya, she did take up the topic at the wrong time, which was during our fights. Like, she showed her friends and family the birthday card I had made for her and the chocolates sent to her. Is she keeping all these things as weapons to use against me during an argument? Why can't she just tell these things to me which would make me feel better and special? The reason might be that I am no longer special for her.

After a tiring presentation and the party after that, I was finally packing my bags for the trip back home. I had a fun time with all my friends here; we drank a lot and partied like hell. I would really miss the company of many out there. I could never forget the times we played cricket in France. There used to be crowd gathered at the grounds to watch and understand the alien sport. I spent the last few days shopping and spending the money that I had earned during my life in Paris. I ended up using up all the money that I had earned from Paris, and also started borrowing money from quite a few people as well. The reason was my sister's marriage in India. All my family members and distant relatives would be their for the wedding, and they all would expect me to bring something or the other for them, as it's not a common thing to have a relative in France. But the fact is that I wasn't earning anything in five digits. I was just a student who had his mind and soul stuck on a girl in India.

I got on to my plane to India. It was our good old Air India. The reason for me taking the risk of travelling in Air India was the baggage limit, those people provided for Indian students. We were allowed to carry a whopping 60kg on the flight and it was a direct flight, so we didn't have to take the burden of getting down at certain airport and go through the menace of security check. But the drawback was the tremendous amount of time I was made to wait in New Delhi. I had to wait half a day in Delhi airport before I made my way to the next plane to Kerala, where my cousin sister was getting married. This was certain period in my life when I took my mind off Anisha and had some fun. Meantime, I had also made a plan to visit Anisha as I was anyway going to Kerala. My trip to Kerala was a memorable one, as it was after a long time that all the cousins in our family got together.

The only difference that it made was that we drank for seven days in a stretch, alcohol from different parts of the world flowing in our blood, starting from country liquor of Kerala to the branded ones of France. The very first thing we did after picking me up from the airport was to go to a bar. We all were totally drunk by the time we reached home. It was a grand welcome that people gave me. After all, I was the first post graduate from the family. I did have other records in my name such as being the first engineer of the family. I personally don't take the credit for that; it was never my first choice. Actually, I never had a choice. Right from my childhood, whenever people asked my father about his qualification and job, he used to say that he was a mechanical engineer and had a business of his own. And these people obviously would be targeting me next by asking about my aspirations in life. I used to repeat the same, saying, I would also want to be a mechanical engineer like my dad. This answer used to make the one asking question, happy and used to further add that I would be doing this to look after my dad's business. So listening to all those reactions over the year, I just chose to be an engineer. I never gave a thought as to what I wanted to become and what I was good at. But once I finished my graduation, I realized that I was surely not a good engineer. Leave good aside, I was a bad engineer. But I believed that I was a good manager, as my communication skills were good. So I could convince most of them out there, of where I did my post graduation, and the area of my interest. But other things were in store for me or at least I thought so. The marriage went well, our family made sure that it was one of the biggest and the best in the town. Money just flowed in for everything, right from costumes to halls and even on our unofficial dowry. People no longer call it dowry; it is just a show of one's wealth and social status. Everyone in the family slowly started going back. Even my parents left for Gujarat, once the marriage was done and we were done with all our after marriage rituals. I waited so that I could make a visit to the academy were Anisha was undergoing some of the toughest military trainings in the country. She had not called for a few weeks, so there was no way I could have informed her about my visit. It was a long eight hour journey from my place, so I felt it was a big risk, as I had no idea about the situation at the academy, whether friends and family were allowed to visit them or not. But I just took the risk. I had even called Aditya, staying near the academy, to pick me up from the train station and take me to the academy. I had a wonderful time with Aditya; we had a lot to catch up after college. He was witness to all my affairs and dramas in the college. I had breakfast from his place before leaving for the academy. On meeting his family, I realized where this Harish Chandra Aditya was from. His family were very hospitable and I had a very good time there. I had to give Aditya a background of things between me and Anisha as I hadn't told him anything about her and now he was seeing me travelling on an overnight train to visit some girl, I had never mentioned about. So it was obviously necessary. I told him that she was just a friend of mine.

It was really a tense moment till I got into the academy. We got lost in between and also had to pass through many police check posts, I shouldn't have expected any less security for Asia's largest naval academy. I didn't have a clue as to what to do, once I was in that place. I didn't even have an address. All I knew was that there was a trainee in this academy by the name Anisha who happened to be my cousin. This was what I had to mention in order to pass the dozen check points. I reached the area were relatives and family come to meet their loved ones. There was a system through which one could make an announcement and get the person, one wanted to the visitors' room. I waited for a few minutes, and then I saw a thin dark complexioned girl running towards me. It took me a few minutes to digest what I was seeing. Academy had snatched away the word beauty from her dictionary. There were all injury marks on her skin; her palm and skin were so rough. I never felt I was touching a girl. And to top it all, she was wearing a shirt and pants which were of my size, I guessed. She was made to look in such a way that even the most despoz would be turned off. I didn't see much joy in her face on seeing me. I felt it was mostly because of the environment she was in. She had to be well disciplined and control her emotions. But there were something that saddened me then. Her so called close friend Raj and his mother were also there in the visitors' room. He was the guy, people used to link her up with. Most of the time during our conversation, they had their sign language talks and smile. She did spend some time with Raj's mother and then came back to me. We talked for a while, but her concentration was more on Raj's mother who visited them every week. I just realized that it was time for me to go back; I shook hands with her and left. She went back to the visitors' room and was continuing her chat with Raj's mother. I had my eyes filled with tears when

Aditya asked me about her, but I couldn't cry in front of him and show the new side of me. But I did tell him everything, once we reached his home, but I didn't cry. I saved all the crying till I got into the train back home and everyone was asleep. Anisha did call me at night; she thanked me for all the chocolates and for coming there. I didn't tell her about my feelings about being treated so coldly as I knew there would be an argument as she would have something to justify herself. I got back home the next day and booked tickets for going back to Gujarat. It was time for me to pay some attention to my career side. I had an interview with a university in Kerala and got myself a job before I left for Gujarat. I really didn't want to get stuck in Kerala, so I was desperate to get a job in Gujarat.

By this time, Anisha passed out from her academy and was on her way to her next training facility which was Cochin. Sometimes I used to think that if Anisha's training period lasted for a year or so in Cochin then I could easily agree to the job they were offering me. But unfortunately, it was just for a period of one month, so there was no way I was going to accept the job. But I made some excuses to make myself available in Kerala during the time. I never realized that I was wasting time and my career on something that was never meant to be and would hurt me in every phase of my life. But still I was dumb enough to go back to her. I was turning out to be a good example of those jerks, blind in love and ruin their life. But it is actually easy said than done. I even gave the same advice to friends around me hoping they would act practically, but no one does act practically in love. Under all sorts of negativism, one always has a positive ray of hope. It was as if destiny wanted to show me how it feels to be hurt in love and how pathetic one could act when he is madly in love. I was shown that in this phase no consolation or advice helps. I was made to feel the pain it causes when you turn a mockery out of your relationship due to mood swings. I respect Shreya all the more at this phase of my life.

A NEW PLACE &
A NEW BEGINNING

Looking at all the late night phone calls, I made during my last visit to India, my parents feared that I would soon find a girl for myself and they always had a fear that it would be Anisha, so they were coming up with a damage control of their own. They were planning to get me engaged soon. Seeing Anisha's attitude towards me, even I thought that I should probably have a last meet with her and then tell her about my parent's plan and just settle things once for all. I finally convinced myself to move on with the flow and right now the flow was taking me away from Anisha. We thought of meeting at around 11 in the morning next day near her academy. She had agreed to spend the whole day with me. I was getting a very good vibe of things to come as if we were getting back to our old selves. I took almost a day to plan everything as I wanted everything to be perfect. I almost played the complete day in mind and assured myself that everything was going to go just perfect. But it has always happened with me that whenever I plan something and play sequences in my mind, it never turns out that way. My schedule included leaving for Cochin in the morning at eight. Meet up with Anisha at ten. She was bit hesitant about ten as she wanted to go to the parlour and do all those routine craps that girls spend hours doing. Then I thought of taking her to the nearby amusement park. It was such a wonderful place and it was a working day, so we would find minimum crowd at the usual jam packed place. It would be a perfect romantic setting. Then in the evening I thought of taking her to the nearby beach resort and enjoy the sunset and have some drinks and dinner. It was to be one perfect day for both of us.

My planning started to take up some modification right from the beginning. Anisha delayed our meeting by an hour as the seniors gave her some work to complete. I was a bit upset but didn't want to spoil my mood, so still thought of making things right. I called Anisha on my way to Cochin and I found out that she was still in her room and she would require a few more hours and asked me to pick her up by one. I got so very upset, but still held on to my temper as I just asked for one bloody day and this is how it turned out to be. I clearly felt the lack of commitment from her side and then realized that she was just another friend of mine and I was almost going to tell her about a relation that my parents were setting up for me. I held back my emotions and drove the car, but this time at a slower pace so as to compensate the delay that Anisha had made and the other big change in my plan was that I had to skip the amusement park from the day's schedule and thought of spending time at the beach. I waited for an hour or so at the marine drive walking aimlessly through the walk way to pass my time till she would be free.

I did get a bit lost while trying to find her academy or to be specific the parlour inside her academy. I waited there at the gates for her and after several phone calls to identify our exact meeting point, I saw her. She wore a white t-shirt and blue jeans to compliment her t-shirt. It was very simple but yet smart. She really had a makeover from the time I last saw her. She was actually looking good, wouldn't be anywhere near the old Anisha but still better than the one in the academy. There can be another possibility that after seeing her in the academy, I had no expectation regarding her look that a slight improvement felt like magical to my eyes. Her clean heart shaped face with soft eyes made me fall in love with her all over again. Her black dense hair were left flowing and not bound to any band, just as I liked. And she always had her endearing and cute character which enhanced her overall personality. She sat next to the drivers' seat and started apologizing with her cute puppy like face. All the anger completely vanished from my face seeing her cute apologetic face. I did tell her about how I had so many things for her and couldn't do it because of the delay from her side. She was very happy seeing the effort I was making, but she insisted on our not wasting the remaining time and would go to some nice place, so I thought of taking her to the less populated and beautiful beach of Cherai.

We did not have anything to eat from the morning, so hurried ourselves to a beach side resort and had lunch from there. It was a perfect setting as we were the only two in the restaurant, as we reached there, way pass the lunch hours. I ordered her favourite chicken and rotis, and also ordered a beer for her. I couldn't drink as I had an important duty of driving and in Kerala it was pretty strict regarding drunk and drive. She wasn't particularly happy with the information I gave regarding marriage proposals, but she remained calm. She did hold my hand during the complete drive towards the resort. Even while having lunch, we sat next to each other holding hands and enjoying the time we got to spend in each other's company. I was being dragged to the days we had started seeing each other. They were one of the passionate and memorable days in my life. She was feeling a bit dizzy as she had the bottle of beer. One noticeable attribute of hers is that she only gets drunk with people she knows and trusts well and I believe I was ranked among the top few, so she enjoyed her drink well. We sat on the beach after a wonderful meal. She was bit hesitant to go out in the sun because she was already made to do that 24*7 in the academy. It was with me she had the liberty to say no and sit in the cool air conditioning of the car. All the time she held on to my hand and was sitting with head resting on my shoulders. We talked a lot about our past, present and the situation of no future. I did agree to all that she said with a lot of pain. After a while she took out her lip balm, I did remember how she used to bring exotic flavoured lip balm and she had to apply after every ten minute interval as it wouldn't be there on her lips anymore. But this time I didn't think of any of that and was busy setting up the internet on my laptop as she wanted to check all the social networking sites and she was totally disconnected from all of that after joining the academy, but the sad part was that I was not able to connect to the internet as the network was pretty weak at the place. It was obvious, as it was pretty far away from the city premises and on the beach. But as soon as I turned towards her, a sting of cold wave brushed through my body, it was as I was electrocuted by some one but a sweet electrocution. I could taste the old cherry flavoured lip balm whose taste I had forgotten in the last one year. It was obvious, after one year of distance; the relationship had its drawbacks. I didn't let her go and didn't think of all the painful discussion we had few minutes back. I just enjoyed the moment as did she. That particular kiss brought a ray of optimistic feeling back into my mind. I started feeling that Anisha still loved me and she did but was pulling herself back due to some unknown reason. No matter what the unknown reason was, I was going to overcome that and win her back. The feeling of love is so remarkable that it just needs a small gesture from your loved ones to make you forget all the corrupt thoughts and disturbing feelings you have about him or her. I was reenergized and was ready to give in one more shot at Anisha. We kissed quite a few times that day after that. I was recollecting the cherry flavour in my mind for good. It was like the camels that go out for desert safari. They actually do not know when will they find the next oasis or water so they make use of the available resources, even though they do not require that at the moment and store it in their hump as fat and utilize it when required. I was storing the cherry in the form of memories and would recollect it whenever I missed her.

There are certain factors that form a romantic evening such as sunset, food, flowers, and chocolates, and I was blessed with most of them. First of all we enjoyed the beautiful sunset, holding hands and walking round the beach. On our way back to the city, we played and sang some of our favourite songs, some were romantic and others were party ones. The mood and ambience was set for something special, but the place and surroundings were bit of a distraction. But we both were always in love with constraints. We never had the opportunity to meet in public, because of the way we both started seeing each other. Our love machine was our only support. She made the ambience beautiful, no matter how disturbing and noisy the surroundings were. We parked the car on our way to the academy and sat for a while holding hands. She slowly bent forward and lied on my lap. She always did that, so that I could pamper her and play with her beautiful locks. I slowly caressed her neck which was the most sensitive part of her body. She immediately went into her shell, once I touched her neck. She closed her eyes and rubbed her head against my lap, which seemed she was struggling to get my hand off her neck, but in reality she was enjoying it as I did. By the time I slowed down my hand, she opened her eyes to find me having a go at the cherry flavoured balm. This went on for quite a while. She was all the time very anxious and careful as we were on the densely populated city premises with people passing by our car every now and then. But the good thing about the Indian cities is that, people are so obsessed with themselves and their work that they hardly have time to look around and enjoy things like the ones happening in our car.

We had a great romantic evening in each other's company and then I drove her back to her academy. A feeling of reassurance and confidence was what I could perceive from her actions today. All was not over between us. It was very late by the time I got back home. It was one of my unforgettable dates, not because of the way we went about the whole day, but because of the notions and messages it conveyed at the end of the day. The message was clearly of love and emotional attachment towards one another.

The meeting in Cochin changed my outlook on our relationship. I was a bit more positive and wanted things to work out between the two of us. I started to call her up more often and we tried to talk like old times. I use the word try, because there are certain things that had not changed between us. She was still equally or even busier than earlier, her coldness while working also remained the same. Perhaps it was me who had changed, she was still acting the same and treating me the same way, but I was ignoring all these facts after the time we spent in Cochin. Even during our conversation in Cochin, she used to say all the wonderful words, but at the end of each sentence the word "but" emerged. It was like she loved me but. It was as if she was preparing me for something big. It was time for me to go back to Gujarat in search of a job. I tried my best to make Anisha visit my home town before I left. She even tried to do so but couldn't get the time, because of her busy schedule. So I thought of meeting her when I caught my train from Cochin. I thought of leaving a bit early, meet up with the proposed girl, whom my parents brought about, convince her to move out of this proposal by telling her about my state of mind. I would openly tell her that being with me was suicidal as I already had a screwed up state of mind and I would really don't want to drag anyone along with me.

The meeting with her went for a bit longer than I expected. I had actually planned to have lunch with Anisha as she would treat me for her admission in the defence forces. But as she said that she would join her friends for shopping afterwards, I thought of preponing the meeting and then meeting up with Anisha after her shopping, so that I could spend more time with her till my train arrived. But that actually turned out to be a bad plan, and in some way good too as I got to see the true colours of Anisha.

Once I wrapped things with my proposed girl I rushed my way back to the station, where I could leave the remaining baggage. I called Anisha on my way to the station to inform that I had wrapped up the meeting earlier and was on my way to meet her. But what I heard on the other side of the phone was not pleasant at all. She said, she was with her friends in a mall and were checking the time for the next show of a particular movie, this really pized me off. I just didn't ask her anything else and banged the phone. I had taken all the efforts to wrap things up with her, so that I could spend more time in Anisha's company, and when I was done with all that, I got to know that Anisha had plans for a movie with her friends. She tried calling me back so many times but I was so upset that I didn't feel like picking up the call. I did think of taking it once in between, but then I realized that I had been played with for quite a lot. This was the time I stood the ground and made things move my way rather than let her control the mast of the ship. I always knew that nothing went according to my plans when it came to me and Anisha, but this was too much, and it was high time I did something about it.

I finally took her call hoping for an apology from her side, but instead what I got was more insult and more anger justifying her actions as always. I really wanted to blast her at the same time, but I didn't want to spoil the day, so kept calm and asked her to meet me, as I wanted to give her a sweet that I had prepared on my own before leaving home. It was my first go at one of the most complex sweet dishes of Kerala cuisine and fortunately it came out great. Everyone who tasted it loved it and was craving for more. I had packed the major part of that sweet for Anisha and her friends at the academy so that even they could have an idea about my true talent in cooking. I wanted to gift her that, so took up all the shit told by her and the attitude shown by her. The most amazing part of all that was, she was still able to justify all her anger on me rather than accepting the fact that she didn't like me giving time to an unknown girl over her. It was something that hurt her ego more than feelings. She could openly accept that fact and she was covering that up very well by blasting me for the mistake, I had done. I do agree that I wasn't perfectly right in changing our scheduled lunch, even though I knew that Anisha was busy, but I made sure that she got enough time for shopping. The so called movie was never in her list of priorities till that afternoon. It was something purposely brought about in order to hurt me for hurting her ego. I almost cried begging her to come and just take the sweets from me. It was a bit embarrassing for me, sitting for long at a crowded coffee shop alone. The scene was like, all the people sitting there were with their friends and loved ones and laughing out loud, some flirting and others just enjoying some good time together. But in the midst, there was me who was waiting for someone who probably wouldn't turn up, because her ego was hurt and she was insulted in front of her friends. Even I would have done the same if one of my friends or acquaintances had insulted me likewise in public, but this was different. She was something more than a friend to me, but that was not the case with her and she, for the first time in these two years, admitted and said that openly to me. She blasted me saying that I couldn't expect her to do or come to places that I wanted as she was just another friend of mine and was no longer my girlfriend. It was something unexpected, insulting and more so made a fool of me. I just couldn't look into my own eyes; I couldn't even open my own eyes. It was something that I always knew about her, but never thought she would put that in my face so bluntly.

I have always seen guys do the same, they act like Mr. Nice guy in front a girl and impress her till he gets her in his bed, and after getting laid he would just mind his own business and show cold shoulders to her. I was just feeling the same as that girl at that point would feel. I am not saying that Anisha used me in anyway, but the feeling of being used was there. My statements at this point may seem to be counter opposites, but it was just my state of mind. On one side, I could still not believe that I would ever hear something like that from her mouth and, on the other side, a feeling of betrayal and cheat was running through my blood. I made my way out of the café after a final failed request; I saw a group of children sitting by the street near the marine drive. I went up to them and poured all the sweets, one by one on to their bowls. I was relieved for a while seeing the smile on the faces of those children. Those smiles acted as pain killers for me at that point. It was as if their first meal of the day and that was the biggest appreciation that I had ever got for my preparation. The children thoroughly enjoyed their share of sweet. Once done, they asked me for little more, I just couldn't say no to them, so I just grabbed a bottle which I had kept aside for me and for my cousin, whom I was planning to meet on my way to Gujarat. I poured that bottle of sweets too on their plates and moved on. A little girl in that group stood up and thanked me. I was really touched by the gesture. I thought if Anisha could show even a fraction of the love that little girl showed, then things would have been really different now. Once out from that place, the thoughts of Anisha came back to my mind and I couldn't understand how she could still enjoy the movie after insulting and hurting me so much.

I had never before gone through such a miserable phase in my life, that too in public. No one ever had done anything to me like that, there were many people I hated and people I was not in good terms with, but they all showed a certain level of respect and ethics in enmity. People should learn from her, how to be cold blooded when it comes to hurting someone and that too a person who supported her during the most difficult times in her life, the time when she even thought of committing suicide. I never came up with any excuses in being there for her. It was surely an important phase in my life. I was going through tough simulation classes, lectures and, above that, had to do tough labour in order to earn some extra money. I spent all of that on her so that she never felt left out or alone. She could have at least kept that in mind when she was being blind, she could have left me showing me some respect. All these feelings came out in a very unpredictable and harsh manner. I abused her like anything; I called her things which one should never call a woman. I did not even consider that she was a woman before uttering those filthy words. I always had high regards for women and used to talk about their equality, but forgot all that in an instance and created a totally different image of my own.

I soon realized that this was the end of a dream love relationship for me. After all the abusing got over, I entered the train and started crying like hell. There weren't many people in the train, as the train was starting from that particular station and it had arrived a bit early to the station. My compartment was totally empty for the moment. I made the most of that by crying out miserably. I had no one to talk to and share my pain except the always reliable and trustworthy Anjana. Anisha was an important part of all the dreams and aspirations I had for my future. So, when that important part was left out, I felt my life to be meaningless. All my dreams felt worthless without her. It was as if I didn't know for whom I was achieving all this. With whom was I going to share all my achievements? I abused Anisha the whole night through messages. I believed that it was the way I was surviving the trauma. I was channelizing my anger by abusing her rather than doing something for which I would regret later in my life.

ANISHA

Things did change when I came to know from Anurag that his parents were thinking of getting him married. We were to meet before that, so he came to me at the academy. We had a nice time together and we felt that things might get back to normal, but I was really not into him anymore. I had distanced myself from him by then. I really did not end things up the right way. I was really blunt and straight forward towards a (that) guy who was completely dedicated and into me for so long. But I cared little about that and just broke the news to him. I didn't meet him the day he wanted to, to solve the matter but I chose to go for a movie with friends. He was shattered that day; it was evident from all the abusive words he used to curse me. He was really angry and pizzed and it was clear from his messages he felt cheated. Somewhere I believe that I could have taken it easy on him and shouldn't have been this blunt towards him. I shouldn't have dragged it this far, if I was not sure in the first place. Anyone in his place would feel the same. I didn't reply to any of his abuse as I was hurt myself seeing what he felt about me. He compared me to a slut which was really painful.

ANURAG

It was late at night, the train was jam packed with people travelling to Mumbai. I was not able to control my emotions, so went to bed so that I did not have to talk to people around me. I was still crying, shattered and lost hope in everything that I did till then. I found my existence meaningless. I did think for a while that I was crying for a girl that I met two years ago and I was planning to end my life for her. I was not thinking of my parents who had been part of my whole life. Things that I was doing did not sound practical and this is what one calls love, it is never practical. I didn't feel like sleeping, I was so tempted to just jump out of the moving train but something was holding me back. I didn't feel like sleeping, so got out of my bed and went and stood near the doors. The train was really moving fast and I was just admiring the landscapes in the moonlight. I kept on staring outside the train for long, I waited till midnight so as no one disturbed me in between, and even the clerks of the air conditioned coach were sound asleep. Just then the train slowed down near a small isolated station. There I saw a station master waving the green flag allowing our train to pass.

ANJANA

Seeing the dedication and effort Anurag was putting, I always feared that if this didn't work out then Anurag would be shattered and would go in to a state of trauma from which it would be nearly impossible to bring him out. He had given his everything for her and all his dreams and aspirations revolved around her, and her absence from his life was going to bring everything crushing down to the floor. And all my fears did eventually come true. He was shattered, silent and had gone back to his shell from which he had come out with great caution. It took a lot of time to bring out this Anurag in him but it all disappeared in a flash. I tried my max to be with him in this miserable stage by texting him 24*7. I kept my work aside and prioritized this issue, as I knew the depth of its consequences. Anurag was in a disturbed state of mind and was capable of taking some drastic step, which he would repent. It was all of a sudden, during the day he was excited, as he said he would be meeting up with Anisha and by night what I heard was that he had broken up. I am sure that Anurag's anger would have a role to play in the road to these incidents.

I had talked to Anisha a few times when she was in Bangalore; we had plans to meet up but couldn't manage time. But from what little I could know her; she seemed to be a very nice girl but shared some behavioural trends as Anurag, which would be anger and ego. It was difficult to manage a relationship with people of same trends. But during the past few months, Anurag had changed a lot, he was able to control his anger to quite an extend and it was obvious for whom he was doing so. I haven't seen Anurag love anyone so madly. I was really upset for him as I couldn't be with him when he needed me the most. He was giving hints of something weird and peculiar. I was really not able to understand them, but things didn't sound right. He was having some sort of suicidal temptation within him. These feelings and notions were never expected from a guy like Anurag. This showed the depth to which he had dedicated himself to Anisha.

Anurag some how got into the train that night, he had all the weird thoughts in his mind and was talking of suicidal temptations again and again. I rubbished those discussions and asked him to think on practical lines. He was crying very badly and so asked me to leave him alone for sometime, as he was going to sleep. He still had the ego in him which stopped him from crying or breaking down in front of me. He felt it to be embarrassing to cry in front of me. I knew him well, so thought of leaving him on his own for sometime. I felt he would be back to normal after a good night sleep, but destiny had something else in store for him, I never heard from him after that. I didn't bother disturbing him that night, so just messaged him to take care of himself. I did try to call him the next morning but no one answered the phone. It was switched off. I called his other number, as he used to carry two phones, but the same result. I did get a bit worried after all the things that he told me in the night. Many things came in to my mind within a fraction of a second. I immediately went cold. I tried reaching his phone again and again, each time hoping that there would be someone answering the call on the other side and would tell me that he was sleeping and so couldn't pick the call, but it never happened. I tried reaching his parents after waiting till evening, but got the same answer from them. His mom picked up the call this time; it was evident from their sound that things were not that well. I could just imagine their situation as they did not know the things that led to their son's sudden disappearance. For them it was like one fine morning they were not able to contact him. I tried reaching Anisha as if she might know something or if he had messaged her after that, but she was equally shocked hearing this news. I didn't wait to console her and all but continued trying every means to find him. I waited till late night when his train actually reached his station, but it was later that I came to know from his parents that Anurag was not there in the train. He got off the train somewhere at night and now he was missing. There was no one among his loved ones who knew his whereabouts and what had happened to him. Everyone was just praying that he didn't do anything stupid. I always believed that he was just taking a break from his present world as he was feeling choked in the surroundings and he would return back home soon. This wait has been going on for the last one month. I really wouldn't want to blame Anisha or their relationship for what has turned out, but sometimes I cannot help it. Things would have been different if everyone had acted maturely and handled things differently, But . . . . !!!

ANISHA

After a day passed, I saw that his messages had stopped; I felt relieved and thought of leaving him on his own, as my interference would only make matters worse. By night fall, I got a call from an unknown number, it was Anjana. I had earlier talked to her, but hadn't saved her number. She was Anurag's best friend; I thought she wanted to resolve our issue which I was nowhere interested in. Anjana sounded bit worried and the first thing she asked me was if I got any call from Anurag after yesterday; I declined and asked about the matter. What she said was shocking and terrified me to the core. Anurag was missing. My attitude and bluntness had destroyed a life. I really didn't know what to do next. I was shell shocked at the moment and was trying to get back my senses. I tried calling him the very moment but it was switched off. I was sure that this would have been tried out by his friends and family.

I prayed that he shouldn't do anything stupid, as that would shatter me forever. The only mistake that he had ever done was loving me. He never forced or compelled me into anything. The one who should be punished is me and not him. All the professional achievements that I would ever gain would have the smell of cheating and betrayal, which I did to a guy who was once silent and family oriented. I brought in newer priorities in his life and changed him, which people believed was for the good, but it all came down to this. It was a huge price he paid for changing himself. I dragged him in to my confused life and shattered his almost perfect life. I have had made quite a few mistakes in my life which includes acknowledging his love for me. I was never satisfied with the love and affection I received from my loved ones and always compared each with others. I learned my lessons the hard way and sacrificed Anurag in the deal.

ANJANA

It was like the circle of life got back on to Anurag but this time he was on the receiving end. Anurag got a taste of what he did to Shreya. It made him realize how difficult it was for Shreya and how she took the pain and moved on in life which Anurag never could.

IN THE BEACHES OF GOA

I had no clue as to what I was doing then; it was all in at once. I felt like getting off the train and I just did. I was not that melodramatic to forget to take my luggage and iphone with me. There was every chance that within a few hours I would realize that it was a dumb idea to get off the train. But I was determined from within to just throw Anisha out of my life and prove to her how well I could do in her absence. Easier said than done, I had a mammoth task in front of me.

I already knew that I had got off at some stranded ghostly stations of Goa. It was Goa and the first thing that rang to me was Gaurav. The last time I had talked to him, he was living with his girlfriend in Madgaon, Goa. He has always been a rebel. He loved doing things his own way, had made quite a few mistakes and ended in trouble most of the times, but he still kept on doing it, that's why people loved him. He didn't change himself for anyone. You may love him or you may hate him but cannot ignore him, and I really cannot afford to ignore him in this state. I believed he was the best person to consult at the moment, no one could explain love better than he. I wanted to cross check for his current phone number, as I didn't want to disturb someone else at this point at night. So I went to the most popular place for the emotionally traumatized, not the bar this time around, but equally efficient "Facebook". I checked up his details and called him up and informed him about my whereabouts. He sounded bit worried as I called him at a very odd time. I wouldn't be surprised, as anyone would react the same way if someone called at 2 in the morning and said that he was standing at a railway station nearby, so please pick him up. I made sure that I called him from a public phone booth as I didn't want people come looking for me by tracking my phone number.

While I was waiting for him at the station bench, I just went back in time and remembered the fight I had with Gaurav. It was for the first time I had a physical fight with a friend of mine, that too a guy who had been my roommate and partner in crime for the whole college life. I just laughed at myself realizing how silly our fights were. That day when we raised hands against each other, it was for a cricket match. Actually we didn't raise hands; it was the bats that we raised against each other and a few minutes later we were on the ground with a big tussle and people trying to pull us apart. I really had a history of hot headedness and making dumb mistakes. But actually that fight helped us bond; we were much closer to one another from that day. It was always Adi who shared the tag of my best friend from college but the true experiences of college life, I shared with Gaurav. It was me and Gaurav who were wandering around to get a rented house and finally the house that we got was so expensive that we had to put in all the money we had in the bank. The real estate agent was so moved by the situation that he bought us food that day, it showed the extent to which we were broke. All these thoughts brought in a smile on my face and for a few well cherished moments, I forgot about Anisha and the trauma I had just gone through. Just when those thoughts came buzzing in to my mind, I felt a pat on my back and it was Gaurav. I didn't say anything but hugged him and broke down. He calmed me down and took me home on his bike. It was nice to see the good old Gaurav. He didn't question me once on the way; he just took my bag, tied it on the back of his Royal Enfield and drove off. It was good that he didn't question me then, because I was more worried about his driving, because during the college days, it was on my bike that he learned driving and I exactly knew his expertise with that piece of machine. For a moment I felt that it should have been better in that train.

I had a few shockers once I reached Gaurav's place. First and foremost, Gaurav didn't have a girlfriend anymore, she was his wife now. Her name was Kritika, a doctor by profession. Gaurav, the rebellion proved his tagline right when he moved out of his house to marry her. She was waiting for us at the gate, she was a nice girl. It should have been like that, after all the trial and errors he had had with respect to girlfriends. He finally had to get it right someday. I just had a glass of water and a small chat with Kritika and then Gaurav dragged me to a small well furnished room which was his so called library. Gaurav was very fond of reading right from college days but his tastes of books were mostly Debonair and GQ. But things do change with time, Gaurav; the Romeo from college is now an engineer and works at the port. As soon as we entered the library, I joked about his interest in books, but he was in no mood for my jokes, he wanted to know what led me to this place in the middle of the night with no prior notification. It was clear that it was no leisure trip. Gaurav was also part of my smart work team from college or one can say the bit team. So I considered him smart and so he would obviously make out. I explained to him everything that went on from the day I passed from college. At some point he was really proud of me and at some, very disappointed. Once the narration was completed, I looked on to his face. It was expressionless at the first glance. He went into some form of shock to understand my rogue decisions I had taken in the past few months. He used to think himself to be the king of dumb decisions but he accepted defeat. He was also shocked at one more thing, my love for Neha. He couldn't believe that I kept it to myself for four long years of college. The only word in the dictionary he felt suited me was "Jerk."

He arranged the bed in the guest bedroom and asked me to take some sleep and then have a discussion in the morning. My morning started with a cup of coffee from Kritika and she was giggling at the time she handed over the cup. I realized that her indefectible husband had narrated my complete story to her. I met Gaurav on the breakfast table. It was a self service routine because by this time Kritika had left for work. I had a serious discussion with Gaurav on the breakfast table. The first thing he asked me to do was to inform my parents about my whereabouts, as they would be perturbed by now having no info about me from last night. I said I would do so once I fetched a job for myself in this town. I went with Gaurav to his office, as he was very much adamant that he wouldn't leave me out of his sight. I even got a chance to browse the internet for some job search. Life was really calm and serene in this beautiful town. People here had much more to life than money. They understood and valued their life. They enjoyed what was given to them. I started liking the vibe to this culture. Gaurav and Kritika were really supportive and hospitable at home. We used to spend evenings at the beach admiring the sun going down. The very sight was mesmerising. After a beautiful day the sky is blue with just a few clouds. The sun starts to go down with a yellow, orange and red hue. The sun is bright yellow; the clouds turn a purple and gray. It looks like the sun is burning things, as it sets and sizzling the water in the sea till it is boiling. In a matter of just minutes there is nothing but darkness or an orange or almost red coloured moon. I realized that I had started cherishing and enjoying the small things in life, which one ignores or takes for granted. After a few days of job search and resume sending, I finally got a call from an engineering college. They were looking for someone to teach in their department. I never knew when I sent an application to the college. I still don't get it how I cleared my papers and now here I am, shortlisted to be teaching hundreds of aspiring engineers. As I once said, this country is in deep shit. Anyhow I was desperately in need of a job, as I couldn't take Gaurav's hospitality for granted. The college was providing accommodation for its staffs, so at the moment it looked like it was the path in front of me and if it meant sacrificing a few young minds to get what I wanted, then let it be. Looking on the brighter side of it, I was getting a chance to learn things which I couldn't a few years back. Who knows, I might end up an engineer after all.

I informed Gaurav about this opening; firstly we had a laugh about it remembering all our teaching staffs that treated us as Ginny pigs to polish their teaching skills. Gaurav believed it was time to return the favour and pass it on to the coming generations of the so called engineers. That is why it is said that a person doesn't always become an engineer with the bookish knowledge he has gained, it's his experience that makes him a better one. So let me pass on to them my experiences. Gaurav had some contacts in the area which assured that I would get the job no matter how talented my competitors were. People elsewhere would name it cheating or influencing, but in India it's called Jugaad. So now I was an Assistant Professor at an engineering college, thanks to Gaurav and as always my convincing manners. The first thing that I did after coming out of the college was to call my parents. I called up mom at first as she was the more patient out of the two. I had a better chance of explanation with her. I was bit scared to call her up but gathered strength to do so. I had no explanation for the giddy behaviour from my side.

FAMILY PATCH UP

The long emotional conversation with mom went well. More than being angry with my behaviour, she took a sigh of relief knowing that I was safe and doing well. Even Dad was their beside mom, so even explained matters to him. He didn't reply anything, it was typical of dad. He was the more worried and curious out of the two, but he wouldn't show that. He wouldn't ask me anything but compel mom to do so, so that he could know things about me and breathe easy. So it is obvious as to where I got this attitude syndrome from. My parents did compel me to come back home, but I convinced them regarding the job I got and that I would come back to them soon, but before that I had a few things to prove to myself. I left the family melodrama behind and was busy shifting to my new home. It was a weekend, so Gaurav was helping me with buying all the household basics. The house that they provided was small but yet spacious, perfectly situated in a beautiful residential area near the beach, surrounded by gardens with trees and lot of flowers. It would be warm and light in winter and cold in summer. This house had a single bedroom, a living room, a small kitchen cum dining room, a bathroom and no other fancy rooms such as library etc. The built of the house was partly old and partly modern, a really hi-teach house but all very stylish. It seemed a quiet, safe neighbourhood with friendly people. The place was quite and serene but yet in the middle of things. It was a fifteen-minute walk from the city centre of the town, a five minute to railway station and a ten minute from shopping centre Square. Everything one needs is at an arms reach. The name given to the residential block was apt "Nature's Bliss."

The house near the beach enabled me to continue my evening stroll and the view of the sunset which I wouldn't want to miss. As a customary after moving in to the new house, I invited Gaurav and Kritika for dinner at my place. They both never missed a chance to have dinner prepared by me as they loved it. During the course of time I realized that cooking was one thing, I never got tired of. If someone asked me to do it for a whole day and cook for a group of hundred men all alone, I would still do it happily, because I loved it. Cooking for me was like working in a science lab. I felt as if I was inventing something and I got a chance to mix up all the masalas, and when the end result came out good, it was the best feeling I ever had. I was known for the innovative recipes I used to come up with, and luckily for me, it always turned out good. With every passing day, the bond with Gaurav and Kritika was strengthening and moving on to a new level. I considered Gaurav a friend, I could trust and turn to in the matter of need and Kritika was like a young sister to me. I was building up a new family away from home. Days passed quite fast, I made some good friends at work, but all of them were limited to my work place, no one that special who could cross my imaginary boundaries and get into the protective cocoon. In a way, I was scared to let anyone come close to me. I tried doing it once and it failed me terribly. The good thing about being at this new place was that I was totally away from my past. I didn't see anyone who was connected with my traumatic past, so it helped me move on. I did contact Anjana in between, to inform her that I was safe and was working in Madgaon. She like everyone else scolded me and then left the matter. I made sure that I had minimum conversation with her, not her fault but for my own good. It just helped me stay away from all the complex things in life.

AN IDEA

I had an excellent routine which started with college in the morning and go on till five in the evening. I loved the complete ambience of the college as it made me six years younger. It was nice to be in the midst of all campus action and, this time around, I was in a dictating position as a professor. I had formed a good rapport with the students in the early days itself. After work I used to turn up at the nearby beach shack to have some snack which included some lovely cake from Sam who is the chef at the shack. Company of chefs was something irresistible for me, I used to have chats with him during the evening coffee and share my recipes and vice versa. I used to sit there till sun went down, then I would slowly, make my way back to my room were I used to do some cooking. Most of the days, I used to do the eating at the shack, as Sam would invite me when he tried out some of the recipes that I taught him. He even let me do some cooking at his shack, seeing my interest and knowledge in the area. Sam's shack was one of the popular eat out places in Madgaon. The sea food cuisines with beer would be an excellent way to spend one's night in Goa. It used to be my best hangout place with Gaurav and Kritika during the weekends.

One such Saturday night, we were having grilled fish and some beer to go with it that was when Kritika asked me as to why I didn't start my own shack. Gaurav laughed at this point and I too rubbished it aside, but Kritika was damn serious. And when she was serious, one should better give her the attention she demanded or else its chaos. So I silenced Gaurav and gave an ear to what Kritika had to say. What she said after that did make sense. Anyway all the recipes that I taught Sam were a hit, so there was no doubt in my cooking skills, then why was I not doing it myself? What I earned every month after all the chaotic sessions with the minds of tomorrow was what Sam earned just on a single weekend. It even made sense that I had my eatery just for the weekends and it wouldn't even affect my job. After a wonderful dinner, Gaurav and Kritika left home, I was making my way back home. My mind was preoccupied with what Kritika suggested in the night. My mind started wandering for better ideas and something unique in this eatery business. I wanted something beyond the shacks. That was when the street food vendors of my home town struck me. Back home, my weekends used to go about eating at the street food vendors, which would be jam packed during the nights and one other place where one could find the same magnitude of crowd was a fast food outlet. No matter how pathetic the food taste, you would still find crowd if it had a popular name and if they charged you outrageously. These were the criteria for a fast food restaurant to be a hit. One could find better tastier food for minimal cost at a street food vendor, but one would prefer the expensive chains. What struck me then was why I couldn't combine these two together, a fast food outlet that sold street food. One could even put it the other way round, fast food at street food price.

The very next day, which was a Sunday, I spent most of the time, brain storming on the idea which came in through a little help from Kritika, some input from me and the rest from the irresistible effect of the beer. By late afternoon, I had a clear plan about my restaurant and I called up Gaurav and Sam to discuss about it. Calling up Sam seemed weird as he would be rated as my rival if I was going in to this business, but this was something new that I had in store. The motivation for my restaurant came from Anisha. The core idea of the restaurant had her character in it. The restaurant should be simple, elegant and down to earth but should still carry a sense of panache, typical Anisha. I informed the guys about my plans of starting a mobile restaurant which would be integrated through mobile applications and all. It would be a hi-tech laari. The mobile van would have predetermined halts throughout the city. The van would act as a bus which had stoppage areas with sign boards stating its stop and the duration of its stop. Anyone having a smart phone could find out the current status of the van using their mobile app. They could even pre-book their order and mention their stop through the app so that the van would be ready with the food before it got to the stop and the customer wouldn't even have to wait. The app will also feature facilities like poking which would enable the van to have a rough estimate of the people waiting for them at the next stop. Sam was really impressed with my idea and instantly agreed to play his role in it. The kitchen would be handled by Sam in this case. Sam might not be the most educated entrepreneur but he knew his business well and he could very well understand what would work and what not and, from whatever little he heard about my idea, he felt it would definitely work. I would be preparing the business plan and lead the project in this case. I would use Gaurav's influence in getting some finances and securities for loan. Gaurav had no doubt ever of my money making skills. He knew that I just needed the right push and for now I had got enough reasons to prove myself. It was a go ahead from each of us.

I utilized most of my free time at college in preparing the business plan and the evenings used to be spent at Sam's shack, discussing how the menu should look like and how we were going to present ourselves. During all this planning, I always thought of informing dad about this, but I was scared to do so as the first reaction from him would be that I had taken all the pain in the world to become an engineer and done my masters in Germany so that I could be a street vendor. He was of an old school and I couldn't blame him for thinking that way. It would be difficult for him to see the bigger picture. Gaurav also came up with certain contacts that could be convinced of pooling money and acting as stakeholders. Everyone was doing their part in making this dream a reality. Kritika never liked being a spectator when it came to these situations; she pooled in some money from her savings and got me in touch with a local garage guy who would help me modify my van to make it apt for an eatery. I was really happy with the kind of people around me. Finally I felt things were going my way.

MOVE ON . . .

As everything was falling in line, I felt it was time for me to call up Anjana and let her know about things. I was expecting to launch my restaurant in a month or two, so wanted her to know what was going on. She was happy for me, but our conversation was down to minimum. I wasn't getting the same friendly vibe from her which I used to get. She obviously had the right to be mad at me for not letting her know of things down here. I once hinted that I, after the Anisha fiasco, did not trust anyone around. She was really exasperated on hearing those words uttered by me. Even I felt that it was a bit out of proportion and I should have held back my words. But as always, I think only after uttering some bullshit and later regret over it. Right now I didn't even have time to regret. I was so absorbed with my restaurant work and my actual college job during the day time. Anjana did tell me that Anisha used to call her up once in a while to know whether there was any update about me; somehow I felt that she was not that bad after all. But I didn't want to be carried away by emotions anymore.

Today I realize the kind of emotion Anisha had for her ex boyfriend. Whenever asked about him, she used to tell me that she missed him a lot but didn't want him back in her life. I never understood the logic behind the sentence. I thought, she told me this just to make me feel better and less insecure, because how could one person like the other and not want him back. But I realized it soon when I was in her shoes this time around. It was clear for me that I didn't want Anisha back in my life. Whenever I think of forgiving Anisha, I am reminded of all the insult that I had gone through and the way I was taken for granted and in the end left in utter disarray. But that didn't mean I didn't miss her. I had some of the best time in my life in her company. She changed me for good and helped me enjoy life. I would always be thankful to her for that and would always love her for that. No matter what goes on in my life, I would always love her but that won't change my decision. I wouldn't want to end up with her. Let her be a part of my life, where I had fun, had some cherished moments, then taken for a ride and then left to suffer so that I could come back stronger than ever.

I believed there was something that Anjana was not telling me. I did really poke her more than once but it was of no use. I knew Anjana well. She knew what to tell and when to do so. She would only do so when she felt it was the right time.

KERALA XPRESS

I am getting ready to meet the bank manager today. All my hard work and business proposals are coming down to this day. Today I will be able to decide where I will stand ten years from now. Will it be my dream life or am I going to end my life teaching spoilt brats in an engineering college?

I am very confident with myself. I always used to call up Anisha before something important in life, as I used to consider her my lucky charm. I still do consider her as the one. But the only difference is that I don't call her anymore, reasons are quite obvious and more so because she doesn't believe in my superstitions anymore, nor does she like me calling her anymore. She believes this lucky charm thing to be a childish gimmick.

I took out my phone, went through the picture albums and took out Anisha's picture. I had saved one of my favourite pictures of her in my phone till then.

It was she sitting on a swing and all smiling. I looked at her picture as if I was talking to her, telling her about my meeting today and in return she was smiling, which meant everything would go great. I just kept my phone inside and had a slight hint of smile on my face and an over doze of confidence. I was ready for the verdict. I went to Gaurav's place but Kritika said that he left for Cochin to meet some friend of his. It sounded pretty strange because I knew all his mallu friends and I hadn't heard of anyone from Cochin yet. I am so confident about this because Gaurav is a mallu just because of his parents. He has nothing to do with Kerala or its people. I expect Gaurav to be there by my side on this important day. But anyhow it is fine, as I know Gaurav will be there if it is something avoidable.

Even before entering the bank, I saw Sam waiting for me outside the bank and he came to me and gave a tight hug. I didn't understand what he was trying to say. Actually he didn't, he just smiled and asked me to go in and meet the manager. The manager's approval shocked me. I was rapturous and over the moon with the news. I wanted to tell this to the whole world, but then controlled myself saying that the work was yet to start. It was just an approval. I now have the finances but the actual work is still left. I have to put all my business plans and ideas to practise. I had already started the vehicle modification with the money I got from Kritika. I thought of returning it once I got the loan amount ready, but Kritika refused to take it and rubbished it by stating that she would take the money back in the form of unlimited food from my restaurant so that she had to cook for Gaurav no more.

The date for the inauguration was coming near. I was in touch with all my old chaps from college. It would be a great reunion cum inauguration. The concept of my restaurant was already creating vibe in the town. It would be an all out Kerala fast food restaurant. All rare and authentic recipes from all corners of Kerala were sorted out for the menu. I had taken Adi's help for the same. Adi hails from north Kerala, which is known for its stunning cuisines and that's what I wanted the rest of the country to know. I want people to know that there is more to Kerala than idli and dosa. No matter which south Indian restaurant one goes, all he finds is a dozen forms of idli, dosa and vada. There is much more in Kerala cuisine than those steamed rice products. My aim was to cash in on that other side of Kerala cuisine. Adi was helping me bring out some of the rarest of north kerala cuisine and the recipes to them all; with the help of these recipes we prepared an elaborate menu which had the cuisine and also the detailed history about the origin of the cuisine. It was something never tried before. I wanted people to know in and out about the food they were having. I just didn't want people to love the taste, I wanted them to understand the taste and know what they were eating. I wanted people to appreciate and respect the food at the same time. In the meantime, I never forgot the business aspect of the eatery. I planned certain combo deals which would give attractive discounts and woo in customers. Facebook and other social media marketing techniques were intensively used by the marketing team, which was supported by the technical expertise of Anjana.

I had decided May 21st as the launch date for my restaurant. I started sending invitation. First of which was sent to my parents, then followed my friends and other relatives and finally the ones which were part of a formality. I was eagerly waiting to show dad what I had done with myself in the past few months and how I had worked hard to make him proud. But the news from his side was discommoding. He had an important meeting on that day and he would be unavailable then. He congratulated me for my achievements but wouldn't be able to make it for the function. It was really an upsetting moment for me and couldn't believe what would be so important than celebrating his son's first big professional step. The discommoding feeling eased a bit once I got the same reply from Anjana and Aditya. Now I was getting used to it, I didn't understand how all these guys had important stuffs to do on the same day. I always had this feeling that twenty one was my lucky number. It had proved lucky for me in all my endeavours starting from my school days where I had my roll number as twenty one. This continued during my college days and success followed me even there and from then on I made sure that every occasion in my life should have twenty one attached to it, someway or the other. I called up Gaurav, at least didn't get any lame excuse from him, he said he would be there on time but wouldn't be there to help me out for any pre-program arrangements, as he would be getting back from a meeting on the same day of my inauguration. I didn't push myself this time as at least he was making it for the occasion, unlike my other friends and family. And also Kritika was there to help me with all the arrangements; she was really good with all event management stuffs. The food for the guest was handled by Sam, so I shouldn't be worried about that area, it would be handled with at most professionalism and perfection.

I spent the last few days before the inauguration completely in the garage, where the last minute modification was going on with the van. I was being updated about all the legal formalities and license required for starting the service, and I was making sure that I had fulfilled all the checklists. The website was also ready and good to go. The online marketing had been going on for the past one month and a lot of buzz had already been created in the social media, thanks to the technical head Anjana. I even took a week long break from the college, so that I could do all my last minute preparations and I was not diverted to any other matter. The inaugural function included a small pooja, then releasing the logo of the company, then a half an hour long cultural activities. This was something new for the people of Madgaon. I had arranged typical Kerala style dances and drum processions, namely, *panchari melam* and *puli kali*. It was like a never seen before Kerala style carnival away from Kerala. A lot of hype was created through social media about this event and what they could expect in them. Huge curious crowd gathered just to see what the whole colour and noisy fiasco was all about. I was sure that this would be an excellent platform to launch Kerala Xpress, my mobile restaurant. The name symbolises its fast food nature through the name Xpress and it's all about Kerala, so can't leave that word out of the name, and the whole nature of the restaurant was like a train which had scheduled trips around its predefined routes, so the name Kerala Xpress came about.

HAPPINESS UNLIMITED

I was all ready for the big day, Kritika helped me with the shopping, didn't go for any suite or kurtas. It would really not fit the humid climate of the city. I thought of dressing up with the theme of the day and it was Kerala all the way, so wore an authentic dhoti and a Lenin slim fit shirt. Kritika bought some Marathi attire for herself. I thought of gifting the dress she chose as a token of appreciation for the great help she had been rendering throughout all the dreadful traumatic few months in my life. I was still worried as none of my close friends had made it to the venue yet. Most of them ditched me at the last moment, but Gaurav was expected, but he was yet again in Cochin for some meeting. I didn't like this newly formed business in Cochin. I was planning to bring this to the table, once this hectic inauguration was over. Just when I was getting irritated regarding Gaurav's behaviour lately,

I saw him entering the inauguration venue. It wasn't a huge venue that the one's entering the place would get lost. It was just me and a few dozen friends. We did have a crowd outside the venue to see the cultural fiasco though. But I could see Gaurav was not alone, I could see a female figure walking with him. I was shell shocked; all my worst fears were coming true. I couldn't believe how he could cheat on a wonderful woman like Kritika. I was about to walk to him and blast him when I saw kritika walk to him, and he embraced her and she started talking to the woman next to Gaurav. I really couldn't make out who this uninvited guest was.

I went near to this woman so that I could have a better view of the happenings. This woman seemed to be familiar as I moved closer to her. She had locks of sable-black and they surged over her shoulders. She had effervescent, champagne-brown eyes. They were dew-pond round. She had trout pout lips. They were succulent, sultry and velvet soft. She had a genteel persona. She had a melodious voice and her opulent hair glittered in the beams of the sun. She wore bleached, naff clothes in an out of kilter fashion. She had a sculpted figure which was twine-thin. Her waist was tapered and she had a burnished complexion. A pair of arched eyebrows looked down on sweeping eyelashes. Her delicate ears framed a button nose. A set of dazzling, angel-white teeth gleamed as she blew gently on her carmine-red fingernails. I realized, I hadn't lost my ability in orchestrating details. And it was obvious, no matter howmany years passed by; I could never get tired of describing this wonderful creation of god. The girl was Neha. I couldn't believe my eyes. It was like a déjà vu for me. The first time I ever saw her in her class room, I had the same difficulty in trying to get a glimpse of her. I was among the crowd fighting my way to see who the earthly beauty was, and here I was again six years later trying to get a glimpse of her.

I made my way to Gaurav, he saw me coming and he had a smile on his face. I came near them and shook hands with Neha. She asked me if I had any problem as she came for the function uninvited. I overlooked that statement and said that all my friends were invited for my celebration. Kritika and Gaurav stared at each other and giggled. I saw them doing that and punched Gaurav on his shoulder. I had a small chat with Neha and this happened to be the first time I had ever talked to Neha. I had spoken and described about her a thousand times and yet I hadn't spoken to her till then. We just had a brief conversation as to what we did after college and regarding our current profession. It was pretty simple for her as she had been working, ever since she left college. But things were different from my mind; I was a guy born and brought up in Gujarat, studied in Erode, then went to France and then Again back to India and ended up in Goa. My story couldn't be concluded that easily, but before I could start, she said that everything had been already told by Gaurav. I so hated Gaurav at that point. For the first time I had something to talk about with Neha, and here I saw my so called friend had snatched away that opportunity from me.

The day was not over yet. There was a huge group of people following Gaurav; first in line were Aditya and Anjana. They were also part of this plot of surprising me. The next in line were my parents, I just broke down seeing them, it was the same for them too. I had never seen my dad cry before and I would never like to see as well. But this was the tears of happiness. They all were overjoyed to see me finally and that too at the pinnacle of things. Finally, I was taking on responsibilities and doing something worthwhile in my life. I was finally doing something that made everyone happy. The tears of joy that my parents had in their face were a priceless moment for me and I would trade a thousand Anisha for this. The emotional setback that I had when I got in to the train from Kerala changed my life. I took some rogue decisions but with support from people like Gaurav and Kritika, things turned up on the right side.

The function went great, the dance and musical fiasco were breath taking. It was something innovative, so got the attention which it deserved and what I had planned it would get. Media got a piece of all the action that took place that day and were planning to make it news for the next day with a tagline "New kid on the block." Neha wished me luck for my new endeavour and left for Cochin the very next day. I didn't get to talk to her much, as I was busy being the host of the function and the only little conversation I had was stopped thanks to Gaurav. Everything was going as per planned but I still didn't understand how Neha made her way to Madgaon. On being asked, Gaurav said she was there for some meeting, so thought of making it for something very important in my life. It was difficult to sink in because Neha didn't have the best of opinion about me during college. She hated me back then and thought I was very much self obsessed, which I was a bit. I could sense that there was something not right and I needed to get the answers for them.

NEHA

I never thought of sharing this story with anyone in the world. But maybe now's the time when I should express what I really feel like, being in love with someone, whom I can only dream of but never get. Memory is a way of holding onto the things you love, the things you are, the things you never want to lose. Things around us change so fast that before even realizing our loss, we would have already moved on to the next phase of our life. How strange are those old recollections that haunt us, without our being able to get rid of them.

Today, I feel lucky to have plenty of good friends. In my engineering life, I solved equations of friendship along with several mathematical equations to get a good job, and plenty of good friends and I feel I was good at these equation things. The initial months of my college days will always be special to me for endearing me with my college. I was introduced to a realm of code, where I learnt respect for my seniors, importance of friendship, and live life by my own with hurdles, often called 'ragging' surrounding me everywhere. Even today, I cannot understand how these initial days have clung so vividly and tenaciously to my college memories. During our ragging period that was for two initial months of our 1st semester at our engineering college, we had to follow certain rules and wear the dress code designed for us. This was the time of my life when I met Anurag. He didn't leave much of an impression in his first meeting. One needs many such interactions to know and understand him but in my case it never happened. He was a handsome chap. His cheeks were chiselled like a finely-carved Michelangelo statue. His nose was perfectly symmetrical. His lips were slightly full, the kind that end in a cute little smirk at the corners. The rays of sun highlighted the dimples in his cheeks and chin. He seemed a bit of a cold and attitude driven person at first and I was no less when it comes to those criteria. I always preferred people coming to me rather than me going to them, it had always been like that from the beginning and so did I expect the same from Anurag which never happened. We didn't have much of a conversation but my best friend from college, Anjana, was very close to him. Somehow I didn't like the sound of it. I was bit of a competitive person right from the beginning and it was no less when it came to making friends. I didn't like Anjana being friends with someone who didn't bother to pay attention to me or even put slightest of effort to be a friend of the same magnitude as he was with Anjana. One of our mutual friends Adi used to tease him by my name. Everyday more and more people were coming to know about the teasing thing and frankly it never affected me, don't know why but it didn't. And then the worst thing happened at college. Rumours spread out in the class that he loved me. I also heard that Anurag got pizzed with Adi and they were not in good terms. Now "rumour" is one thing that we don't like at all. True to say, maybe I was enjoying those rumours from the inside, but outside I had to show that I was very irritated. I thought Anurag was also doing the same till the unthinkable happened.

The first year of college went by with these cold war of ours, added with a pinch of jealousy. After a few days into our second year we got our freshers, and the door of enjoyment also opened its door for us to enjoy our college life along with seniors. Most of the 2nd year guys changed their routine life to lead a casual life after the end of ragging period. They were all ready to dip inside the sea of love, and grab the most charming girl to make it their soul mate for the rest of their college life. Shreya, a beautiful, graceful, and distinguished looking girl with large black eyes was the one who pulled in my attention. The sole reason for the attention was that she had the attention of Anurag and I wanted to know the reason for it. Shreya was in good terms with Anjana. Later I came to know that Anjana was helping Anurag with Shreya as he liked her. They had started talking with each other on phone, and the hours of conversation got enhanced day after day. It is said that in a college, the news of friendship between a boy and a girl spread out like fire in a forest. The case of Anurag and Shreya was not different; all had started to predict a dalliance between them. And soon the friendship turned into a relationship and that's when I realized what was wrong with me. I was slowly falling for him, he not paying attention to me and his coldness and attitude only dragged me more close to him, but I felt it was too late for me to realize this thing. This frustration of loosing on something special came out in the form of hatred for him. I used to get annoyed at things which were spoken about him, mainly by his best friend Anjana. I even had some skirmishes with her regarding the matter.

Love stories are made in heaven. Many of these are lucky to survive the tests of time, while others don't survive the harsh lashes. Fate plays a major role in all of these. Love fights back, tears roll down the cheeks and hearts are hurt. Time and again lovers are tested. Love is the most precious thing that can happen to someone. Losing this precious thing is indeed the most painful thing. And I was going through this pain. I lost this love before even tasting it. Most of our college days went by with some hide and seek games. Some show off jealousy and coldness. Most importantly our attitude made sure that we never came close to each other or understand the other well. In this period, Anurag was single again and he did try on girls but I never gave it a thought thinking that he hated me. It was in the open how we both used to abuse each other and make fun of each other and publicly showed off the dislike towards each other.

I always thought that before the college ended, we might talk to each other but it was not to happen. We were obviously friends in social networking sites. I obviously did it so that I could keep an eye on him and update myself about the things happening in his life, and even checked out his pictures once in a while. I used to like many of his posted pictures but never used to comment or like them. We even had the opportunity to travel together, yet we didn't talk. I was kind of used to that gesture.

I'm a lot different right now. And I try to forget him. Maybe I cannot ever do that. I will have to carry on this whole of my life. I have heard enough that "true love is once in a lifetime." Though I know, it might be him, yet I pray to myself that he cannot be the one. I can never ever say to him, "I love you". So if he was the one then I had let go off my chances. The girl who's going to marry him shall be very lucky. I never believed I would ever get a chance to meet him or at least talk to him till I met Gaurav a few days back. He made a surprise visit to my work place, which was really unlike him. I was not a big fan of him from college days. He was funny yet cheesy and I had heard a lot of crazy affairs of his during college days. But now he is happily settled and has a wonderful wife. I still didn't understand why he travelled this far just to meet me. His shocking revelations that day took me aback. I didn't know whether to be happy or to be sad about what he told. It was like a bag of mixed emotions. I was both happy and sad at the same time, which made me blush and cry in front of Gaurav. I was happy to hear about Anurag's feelings for me and sad that I came to know this late. We could have had our set of cameo in the college days. Gaurav did the entire enquiry through Anjana and got out what was there in my heart and then he took it as a mission to let me know about the things happening in Anurag's life and what he told Gaurav about his feelings for me. He invited me to join him for Anurag's big day. I agreed in an instant. I was going mad over meeting him. Finally, I could meet him and look at him with all the love I had for him. Gaurav gave me certain instructions and asked me to wait till Anurag maked the first move. Let him make the most of his second opportunity.

THE SHOCKER

I really couldn't believe my ears. Gaurav said something insanely shocking. Neha loved me all these years. It had been so long since we had last met but still she was madly in love with me. I realized one thing that I was not the only silent mad lover in this world. It was an untold love which evolved and matured with time. I did jump into a series of relationships after college but Neha always held a certain place in my life. It was time for me to let it all out; the best thing in here was that I didn't have to be scared of a rejection, which I had all the time.

I took her number from Gaurav and called her up. I was literally shivering this time. She was no less either. We talked for a good one hour between office hours. I used to neglect my other friends as I was so busy with my new business and here I am talking to Neha during peak business hours. I didn't propose her and all, obviously not on the phone. We both knew each other's feelings; it was a mere formality now to say it in words. I wanted to make it special. I didn't have much work to do this time. Both our parents knew about us, thanks to Gaurav. They are all happy about this relationship. I had a telephonic conversation with her parents and discussed my future plans and my intention to propose her for marriage. They were really happy and excited about the happenings. Even I had the full support of my parents. Usually it doesn't happen because they are not the ones who are very comfortable with this filmy affair. They are old school, so they preferred the traditional way of engagement and so on. But when things start moving the way we want, we start seeing success in everything we put our hand in. I was ready to take in more responsibilities and there was no waiting and trying to see whether it would work out or not. I just want to make this work out. I have learned my lessons and I really don't want to screw up this time around.

THE PROPOSAL

I spoke to Neha's boss, and he conspired with me to arrange a "company meeting", which would feature a "special guest speaker." I sent via e-mail several pictures of her and me to a co-worker of hers, I had written phrases describing her from the day I had seen her. One of her co-workers set it all to music in a PowerPoint presentation, and the wheels were in motion. The presentation showed how I described her when she was making her way from the hostel, how I tried hard to have a glimpse of her through the crowd in front of her class, the lunch we had with friends and everything that I remembered about her. Several others were enlisted to help me pull it off, and no one revealed a thing to her. I still find it hard to believe that she didn't find out ahead of time. The meeting starts and her boss introduces the "guest speaker," and in I come. Fifty people in the room, and more than half of them knew what was coming, but the look on her face was one of complete shock. I describe it as "happily mortified." I began to tell the assembled how much Neha meant to me, and was about to begin the PowerPoint, when I said "some people missing." I stepped out of the room, and came back in with Anjana, Aditya and Gaurav, who had made a secret trip to her office, at my invitation to be there for the special moment. They all sat down on the empty seats which were arranged, and I began the presentation. During the show and my speech, every woman in the room was crying. Neha was smiling from ear to ear, still spinning in a rush of emotion as she knew our lives were about to change, and only for the better. The guys in the room were even a little touched. On my knee, I asked Neha if she would give me the unmatched privilege of being her husband. She was able to squeak out a "Yes," and I still stand in amazement that I get to remain hers forever.

My college life came in front of me in a flash. All I had to do was to tell the same thing to her six years back and I would have escaped the pain I gave and received in the form of Shreya and Anisha. But as it's said, everything happens for a reason and in this case I would have never known how much Neha loved me if I had made the first move back then. Neha waiting for this proposal from me for six long years says it all. I did go through a hell of a ride in the past six years but each and every moment was worth it. I tried finding love in Shreya and Anisha but ended up comparing them with Neha, I did screw up many lives on my way but I am happy to know that they are doing well now. I am going to marry Neha in a month's time. This is what I had dreamt few years back when I saw her for the first time. I chased my dreams and I got the love of my life in return. It just shows that not all love stories end with a but . . . !!!

ABOUT THE AUTHOR

Anup Nair was born in Kerala and brought up in Vadodara, Gujarat where he has completed his schooling. He did his graduation in Mechanical Engineering from Anna University in Tamil Nadu and post graduation in Engineering from H.S Emden/Leer, Germany. He has wide spread interests ranging from traveling, teaching, cooking, writing books and his ultimate ambition is to start a Hotel with a difference.

From the time immemorial humans were searching for answers for the mysteries of this universe, some men were doing this more than others. Animals always tend to enjoy what is available to them at that instant without any worries about past and future. No other creature in this world other than humans search for answers for every thing they see or hear. So if one searches more for these answers he is trying to become more human than others. Anup in all his endeavors may be seeking the answers to the mysteries by looking at life from different perspectives.

—G. Jayan